Eleanor Putnam

A Woodland Wooing

Eleanor Putnam

A Woodland Wooing

ISBN/EAN: 9783744641272

Printed in Europe, USA, Canada, Australia, Japan

Cover: Foto ©Andreas Hilbeck / pixelio.de

More available books at **www.hansebooks.com**

A
WOODLAND WOOING

BY

ELEANOR PUTNAM

BOSTON
ROBERTS BROTHERS
1889

TO

PROFESSOR GEORGE LEONARD VOSE.

A WOODLAND WOOING.

I.

WHAT BETTY SAYS.

THERE were five heads in all, and I was tired enough of looking down upon them. It was all Bob's fault, and the longer I stayed there the angrier I grew. No living boy can be so aggravating, anyway, as Bob Greenleaf when he tries, and he generally tries. I had been staring down upon those heads for quite two hours, and only one who has tried it can have any idea how stupid people can be when one sees only the tops of their heads. There was Lucretia's yellow head, as sleek as a canary bird's; Josephine's bleached puffs and coils, — "the nest of a crazy rat," Bob calls it; there was Theodore's

head "running o'er with curls," — how I do
detest a curly-headed man! — and Theodore's
friend, with no more hair than a mouse, and
what little he did have gray; and, last of all,
there was Bobby's rough brown tousle. My
own hair is just like Bob's, and I hate my own
hair. I almost hated Bobby too, just then, for
putting me in such a fix.

It all came about in this way. Bob wanted
his gun-case mended. Most boys mend their
own gun-cases, but Bob does n't, and his gun-
case always seems to have a rip in it if I
happen to be planning a specially good time.
I was just starting for the horse-chestnut tree,
with "A Pair of Blue Eyes" and some early
sops-of-wines in my apron, when out bounced
Bob from the wood-shed and wanted me to
"just take a stitch" for him. Of course, I
told him I could n't stop, and, of course, he
said I was mean, and banged the wood-shed
door. I did n't mind, for I thought he 'd get

over it right away; but he played me a trick
that I won't forgive him for one while. To
sit there eating Aunt Jane's best pound-cake
and grinning while I was up in that miserable
tree, and not daring to move a finger for fear
somebody would look up and see me!

I had only been up in my perch about half
an hour when Josephine Foster came through
the gate in the hedge, with her brother and
the New York friend who arrived the night before. Bob was in the hammock, and Lucretia
was sewing on the piazza. I should have
thought they might have found other places
enough to take the callers, but no, they must
needs bring their chairs out under the horse-
chestnut, as if there were no other tree in the
yard. Bob knew I was up in the tree, and was
glad of it. He thought it was a joke: any silly
thing passes for a joke with Bob. Then, as if
things were not bad enough already, Bob had
to propose an out-of-doors tea.

Now Bob Greenleaf may deny it all he likes, but of course he did that on purpose to be disagreeable. He knew that they would be a full hour over their tea, and he knew that I should not dare to come down before them all. I shall always be sure that Bob did it on purpose.

I knew they would all agree, and they did. Lucretia and Theodore and Bob set off for the house after the tea things, and Josephine began to entertain her visitors by an account of the oddities and peculiarities of the Greenleaf family. Josephine was always spiteful in a mild way. She owned that Lucretia was pretty, but was afraid that she was rather self-conscious. She told the visitor — whose name is Mr. Hamlin — that Aunt Jane was " good-hearted, but queer; " that Father was a model of an eccentric old village doctor; that Bob was dreadfully young of his age, one of the sort of boys who ought to be caged till he was twenty, — I rather agreed with her there, for the time; and that he had a twin sister, Betty, who was as bad as he, — one of the real old-fashioned hoydens who "set one's teeth on edge, don't you know."

I did not at all agree with her there, and I call it rather mean of Josephine to give a stranger such a bad impression of me. Even Aunt Jane admits that I have improved since last summer, and Lucretia says that when my hair is n't rough, and I have my pink lawn gown on, I am really quite nice. Josephine never did like me; but she was checked in her description of my charms by the appearance of a procession from the house. First marched Bobby, with a little table whose legs shut neatly under it like a dead beetle's; Lucretia came next with a tray; and Theodore followed with a pair of willow baskets.

If there is one thing I like more than another, it is a picnic of any size or kind, and Aunt Jane is famous through the whole village for her cakes and dainties. Every instant I grew hungrier, and every instant I grew angrier with Bob, who sat down below cheerfully eating far more jellied chicken than was at all polite of him, and rejoicing in unlimited almond cake and damson preserves. I abominate tea as a general thing; but even tea seemed pleasant and desirable as the fragrance rose to me through the horse-chestnut branches.

How I did long to throw my book at Bob's head, and startle the placid party lingering so long and keeping me cramped and aching in that hateful crotch!

They finished their tea at last, and Harriet Tuell came and marched away with the dishes, but still Josephine showed no inclination to go. The village boys began to pass the gate on the way to drive home the cows. Tommy Hilborn patted by on leathery brown feet, and was stopped at the lane gate by Aunt Jane with a basket of food for his mother.

Now the cows began to come home, cropping along the roadside as they came. Then Father, in his ramshackle old sulky, creaked up the lane.

I was fairly giddy with sitting so long in that abominable tree, and I could have shaken Josephine until her teeth chattered for sitting there and talking inanely about a young lady she met at Newport who told her that she looked like Nilsson. Nobody was paying the least attention to her, and I longed to tell her so. People never do pay much attention when Josephine is talking.

The katydids were singing in the branches all about me. I felt like a katydid myself, up there among the big, damp leaves. I was tempted to cry out "Bobby-did," in loud and startling tones.

Old Ben Walton crossed the rough common and clambered toilsomely up the wide church steps. In a moment the bell rang out for evening prayer-meeting, and Josephine at last really rose to go.

"Mother will want to go to the vestry," she said, "so I suppose we ought not to stay any longer."

Even then they stopped to chatter at the gate, but I did not mind that. My only thought was to get down from that hateful tree. Bob came slowly across the grass to help me down and to jeer at me. I threw my book and shawl at him and came scrabbling ungracefully down. I was giddy, chilly, hungry, and cross.

"I'll pay you up for this," said I, savagely. "Don't think I'll forget it. I shall just tell Father, and see what he'll say to your keeping me up in that tree two mortal hours, you hateful thing, you see if I don't."

"I don't know how you thought I knew you were up there," said a strange voice with an injured tone.

"I — why, of course I thought you were Bobby," I stammered, with my face ablaze.

"I am John Hamlin," said the voice, an amused voice this time, "and I came back for my walking-stick. Good evening, Miss Betty."

II.

WHAT BOB SAYS.

OF course Betty had to plunge right into the middle of things; she always does. Everybody knows that the preface comes first of all; and I was going to write the preface, but Betty had to start right in and write her chapter without saying a word to a fellow about it, so now the preface has to come in here where it does n't belong at all.

You see, we had always planned to write a novel, only we could not agree about a plot. I wanted an Indian story, and had no end of exciting hunts and fights to put in; but Betty was bound to have a Moorish romance called the "Secret of the Alhambra," with a muff of a girl named Zara, the Tearful, and heaps of minstrels and dungeons and guitars and everything else silly and romantic. So we could n't seem to agree anyhow, and at last one morning we had a downright fuss over it. I was mowing the lawn, and Betty was following me about, trying to make me give in, and I stopped the lawn-mower so often to talk to her that it was ten o'clock before I knew it, and I was late at my lessons with Dr. Rice.

"There, Betty Greenleaf," said I, "now you 've gone and made me late, and the Doctor 'll be cross as snaps, and Father 'll blame me for not finishing the lawn, when it is all your fault. You may write your old novel about nothing but love from beginning to end, for all I care. I shall have nothing at all to do with it."

"All right, then, don't," said Betty; and I flung into the house for my books and went off without another word.

I took the short cut through the Fosters' orchard because I was late, and I found Mr. Hamlin lying in a hammock reading and smok-

ing. He really is not a bad sort of person at
all; does n't think he knows all creation, like
Ted Foster, but treats a fellow with some respect. I rather like him. He put his head
over the edge of the hammock as I came along,
and said that he 'd been fishing in a place I told
him of.

"I caught forty-five," said he, "but I wish
you 'd go with me to-morrow, and we 'll try it
farther up the brook. I 've a couple of rods, if
you 'd care to try one of the new sort."

Of course, you know, I was crazy to get hold
of one of those rods: they are regular stunners;
but of course I was n't going to let him see it,
so I only said I would n't mind going if I waked
up in time. Then he asked me if my sister was
at home. I thought, of course, he meant Lucretia, and I told him she had gone over to
Jonesport shopping with Aunt Jane.

"I meant the other," said he, — " Miss Elizabeth."

"Oh," said I, rather crossly, "she's somewhere about the yard; and see here, her name is Betty. Nobody 'll know who you 're talking about if you say 'Miss Elizabeth.'"

Then I remembered how late I was, and off I went. Of course, anybody can see that it was n't my fault, but when I got home Betty had to pounce on me like a thousand of brick. She had finished mowing the lawn herself, and I went to put the mower away in the barn, thinking that she was right good-natured to do it, when down she came from the hay-loft and took my very breath away, pitching into me about something that I never did at all. Betty always did have that way with her.

"Now, Bob Greenleaf," said she, "you 've been and done it again, and you know you did it on purpose."

"Did what?" asked I, for I honestly had n't the remotest idea what she meant.

"You know what," said she. "Don't pretend

to be so innocent, Bob Greenleaf. I'll pay you up, you see if I don't. First was that horrid old tree, and now you go and send him to find me mowing the lawn with Aunt Jane's old green barège sun-bonnet on!"

Of course I could n't help laughing, for Betty does look like such an awful guy in Aunt Jane's old green bonnet; but after all, I did n't know she was mowing the lawn, and I 'm sure I was n't to blame for the sun-bonnet.

"You know how I hate to be laughed at," said Betty, almost crying, "and he was laughing at me all the time; I could see it, though he was so dreadfully polite. 'That is rather hard work for you, Miss Betty; won't you have an assistant?' Ugh! I hate him!"

Then all of a sudden she began to laugh, and I joined in, and we both laughed, and then we both felt better natured. I told Betty that she was a trump to finish the lawn for me, and that I 'd give in about the story.

"No," said she, "I've thought of a better plan than that. We will start out on something new. You see, Bobby, you'll go off to college in the fall, and this is our last summer of being together quite in the old way; now let us write a sort of journal, — take turns writing chapters, and tell everything that happens just as it comes along. Of course it won't sound romantic, but it will be good fun." '

So that is how we settled it. Betty's will be better than mine, because she always had more of a knack at writing than I had.

This is the way we came to write the book, but it is Betty's fault that the preface comes in here, instead of where it belongs.

III.

WHAT BETTY SAYS.

IT was raining in torrents and by bucketfuls, in great gray sheets, and with sweeping gusts. The orchard was drenched, the gutters were overflowing, and all the spouts gushed like fountains. The apple-trees writhed and struggled in the wind, and if one closed the eyes it was far easier to make the time seem like September than the August it was.

All day long it had been pouring in torrents, and all day long I had been sewing with Aunt Jane. By two o'clock I could endure the monotony no longer; I felt that it was simply impossible to look for five minutes more at Aunt Jane's trim, placid figure and the seemingly endless yards of cambric she was hemming; to hear for another second the "crick!

crick!" of her rocking-chair as she swung mo-
notonously to and fro. I was inwardly con-
vinced that I should go quite mad if I stayed
to hear her say once more, as she had said every
ten minutes since breakfast, "Well, I declare,
it does n't seem to hold up much, does it?
If it was September I should think this was
the Line storm." Once she had varied this to
ask Lucretia, "You don't think this could be
the Line storm, do you, Lucretia, dear, come
by mistake in August instead of September?"
To which Lucretia replied very placidly and
sweetly, "Oh, no, Aunt Jane."

Lucretia was working a bunch of marvellous
rushes upon a square of gray linen. She was
the very picture of unruffled serenity. Lucretia
is not one of those easy and untidy mortals
who take advantage of a rainy day to indulge
in old gowns, horrible slippers, and general
untidiness. Were the sun shining in his bright-
est splendor, Lucretia's attire could be no

neater, her pretty feet no daintier, her hair no more satiny in its smoothness.

But I was this afternoon hardly less tired of Lucretia than of Aunt Jane. I was weary of her pink-and-white profile relieved against the rain-splashed window-pane; of the swinging vase of coral in her ear; of her slender right hand with its gold thimble and turquoise-and-pearl ring. I was tired of the hateful day, and I had kept quiet as long as my nature could be made to submit to it. I jumped up suddenly, with a start that nearly frightened Aunt Jane out of her chair, and left the room in my usual undignified manner.

Half an hour later I presented myself at the door of the Snuggery, as we always have called the room which serves Father as an office, and which has been the general haunt of us all in childish days. I had a basket of wood and my apron full of apples, and these I expected to commend me to the good graces of Bobby, whom I found ensconced in one of the wide window-seats, with his feet on a chair, studying his Latin.

"Look, Bob," I said joyfully, "I've been out in the orchard to the sops-of-wine trees. I knew I should find a lot of apples shaken down in this wind, and the grass was full of them; just see what beauties!"

"Did n't you get wet through?" asked Bob, helping himself from my offered apron.

"Just drenched; but don't say anything about it before Aunt Jane, or she'll want to dose me. Harriet has scolded me, and I've changed my things; so that is all over now. I'm going to make a regular Christmas fire."

"A very jolly idea," answered Bob, "only let me make it. Your fires always fizzle, or else they act as if they were possessed, and snap over all creation."

"Sometimes they behave," I am compelled by the spirit of self-defence to return, as I seat myself on the rug and hand him the necessary kindlings, the sticks of yellow birch, and the great unctuous pine-cones.

I cannot dispute his statement with much vehemence; for it is quite true that though my fires do generally manage to burn, they have a frantic, foolish habit of hissing and exploding, and sending unexpected showers of sparks all about. But then neither Lucretia nor Aunt Jane can induce a fire to blaze decently, no matter what wealth of kindling they expend upon it. Father and Bob build great, hot-hearted fires that are superb to watch and to hear roar up the wide chimney.

"There," remarked Bobby, with a just appreciation of his own work, "that is something like a fire, Betty, and don't you think it is n't."

It was indeed a most glorious fire, and blazed and roared right royally. Without the rain still poured in gray, blinding sheets, but the dear old Snuggery was so pleasant that I no

longer minded the rain. Bob and the fire
filled every dissatisfied longing of my heart.
I sat looking into the glowing core of the
great hearth-fire, and fell into a happy dream,
— mooning, as Bob is accustomed to say.

Bob did not choose, however, to leave me
long to my sweet content. While he had
piled the fire, I had suspended six apples from
nails long ago driven for this purpose on the
under side of the mantelpiece; and the delicious odor they gave out as they slowly twirled
around, growing plump and breaking out here
and there with little glistening bubbles, was
suggesting to me all sorts of tempting dishes
which were about to be served to me in the
character of Queen Elizabeth visiting Kenilworth, when Bob broke in upon the fancy with
a most ill-timed question.

"I say," he demanded, "you have n't finished that book of Virgil, have you?"

"No, Bobby."

"But you promised Father—"

"It is vacation now. Don't bother, Bobby."

"But you were to begin in the Fall all square, and you don't want it hanging over you while we are camping out. You're fifty lines or so—"

"From *vox inhæsit in faucibus*," I finished glibly.

"Oh, that's no landmark," returned Bob; "his everlasting old voice was forever *inhæsiting in faucibus*. Anyway, you only lacked about fifty lines of finishing. Why don't you get your book and finish while I'm plugging? Then afterward we'll play cribbage."

"All right," I said. "This only means that you can't bear to see me comfortable while you have to study; but I don't mind."

So I abandoned the banquets of Kenilworth, brought my battered Cooper from the book-case, establishing myself on the rug with the lexicon between Bobby and me; and for half an hour the silence was seldom broken save by the dash of the rain on the windows, the pleasant snap of the fire, and the persuasive gurgle of the apples as they twirled and roasted on their strings.

"Just find the rules for scansion in the grammar, won't you, Betty?" Bob said at length. "This line is all scanned out there as an example, and I want you to hold the book, and hear me prove the scansion, so as to see if I guess right."

The place being found, Bob contracted his brows for a mighty effort, — a preliminary the necessity of which was but too apparent to me, who never could learn how to scan, and could not even see how anybody else could.

"Now there's *a*, long by authority," began Bob. "*O* short before two vowels."

"No, before a diphthong."

"Well, *o* short before a diphthong; *e* long by position."

"No, by authority."

"*E* long by authority; *a* short by authority."

"No, Bob, by position."

"*A* short by position; *æ* elided for euphony."

"Why, no, Bob; it is n't elided here."

"Then I 'd like to know how in thunder you scan it. I 'm sure I can't, it hitches so. Oh, wait; it is n't elided. I see. *O* is long before a final syllable."

"It is short here, Bobby, by authority."

"There now, by thunder!" Bob burst out explosively, "I 'd like to know if there 's any rhyme or reason in scansion, any way; and what 's the good of it. Now I gave a good square guess at every vowel in that verse, and not one man Jack of 'em all was right. I say it 's all blamed foolishness."

"It is no worse than translation," I returned. "Just listen to this stuff. I 've got the rest of it, but I can't make head or tail out of this."

"Well, what is it?" demanded Bob, with the air of one to whom Fate has already done its worst.

"'Him likewise perchance furious alike impelling, and the spoils of the Egean deity whatsoever by means of madness notwithstanding to be about to be sacrificed.' There, that is the very best I can make out of it."

"Well," returns Bob, with brotherly candor, "you *are* a muff. That's plain enough. Don't you see, ' he also declared himself about to be sacrificed, an offering to the insatiate Egean deity; not caring to live moreover impelled by furious madness, but ready alike to finish and be forgotten.' That is as easy as rolling off a log."

"Oh, of course, when you have been all over it," was my rather ungrateful answer.

"Shy your Virgil over here," Bobby returns, unmoved; "and I'll put up the books while you get the cribbage-board."

And for the thousandth time we settled ourselves on the rug, with the cribbage-board on the floor and a little foot-stool between us. I wonder whether I shall ever be able to play cribbage without feeling myself back in the Snuggery, even though I should really be at the ends of the earth; and whether, too, I shall ever be able to shake off the feeling that I am going to be beaten, with the desperate resolve not to be, which always comes over me when Bob begins to deal the cards. Three times his red pegs had covered the course, while my white ones had not once got in sight even of victory. He was growing most aggressively cheerful, and I was becoming correspondingly sober, with a tendency to be red in the face and short in my tones, when a step was heard from the hall.

"There's Lucretia," I had just time to say fretfully, when her face appeared around the corner of the door.

"Theodore has come," she announced; "and Mr. Hamlin is with him."

"Oh, bother!" was Bob's inhospitable comment; "why could n't they stay at home such a day as this?"

"Josephine is n't very smart," I added, relieving my vexation at being beaten on the first thing that presented itself, "if she can't entertain her own company. He seems to be forever coming over here."

"Josephine has a bad headache. Won't you come in, Betty? I wish you would; it looks so for you always to keep away."

"How does it look?" I began; "I am — Bob Greenleaf, it is not your crib! You call it your crib all the time!"

Lucretia sighed and withdrew, while Bob, who could always prove that any deal was his, proceeded to give me the worst hand that one could imagine. And to complete my vexation, a knave was turned on the cut.

"Two for his heels," called Bob, cheerfully; "I shall have to take that queen out of the crib. I put it there by mistake."

3

"Bob," I cried hotly, "if you do I will not play one minute longer."

And at this interesting moment the door opened, and Lucretia, followed by Theodore and Mr. Hamlin, came walking into the Snuggery quite as if it was the place where company was habitually received.

"It is so damp in the parlor," she explained, "and the open fire here is so cheerful."

"Why, this is no end jolly," chimed in Ted. "Quite like old times, is n't it, Lucretia?"

Bob and I exchanged inhospitable glances, and without a word removed our places from the rug to the window-seat, while Lucretia busied herself in finding seats for her guests. The mention of old times seemed to fire Ted, and he rattled away with Lucretia; so that Mr. Hamlin, being largely left out of the conversation, had no choice but to turn to Bobby and me for entertainment. He came and looked over my shoulder, and when I said rudely enough, "I wish you would n't; you make me nervous!" he only answered, as coolly as possible, "You want to discard your ten-spot." I did n't want to discard my ten-spot, but somehow or other I meekly did it; and the result was that I beat Bob at last. After that I had to be more civil to him, and I must say that he was entertaining. He told a lot of stories, and he told them well; so that the first thing I knew, I was actually offering him a share in our baked apples, which by this time filled the Snuggery with a most appetizing fragrance. Ted and Lucretia ate theirs by the fire, while Bob and Mr. Hamlin and I had a sort of tea-party in the wide window-seat; and on the whole it was well that they came over in the rain, for it was rather jolly, if Bob and I were interrupted, and if Lucretia did say afterward that she was ashamed of me when she came in.

IV.

WHAT BOB SAYS.

IT is all very well for Betty to say it was jolly to have Mr. Hamlin come, for she would n't have beaten me till this time if he had n't stood behind her and told her how to play. She never says a word about the sequence he put her up to. But I 'm sure I don't care; I can beat her any time. Just now I can't stop to write, though, for Fred and I are going up to the Long Brook, and he 'll be here in just about one half a jiffy.

V.

I THRUST my head in at the door, and saw Lucretia twisting up the soft yellow plaits of her hair before the cottage mirror on her dressing-table.

"Theodore is coming up the walk," I said, "and Mr. Hamlin. Is n't it good luck that Josephine has a headache and can't go?"

"Why, Betty Greenleaf!" Lucretia exclaimed reproachfully.

"Well," I returned, "I don't want her to be ill, of course; but you know yourself, Lucretia, that five is a horrid number, and I should have had to tag after, myself."

"Why don't you dress?" Lucretia asked, lightly shaking out her blue lawn gown.

"I can't tell what to wear," I answered dismally. "I had my pink muslin on yesterday, you know, when Bobby and I were caught in the thunder shower. Things always happen somehow to my gowns. I don't see why they never do to yours, Lucretia."

"I am careful, I suppose," returned Lucretia, absently.

She was sorry my gown was ruined, but she was very busy deciding whether to wear tiny gold bells or pink coral roses in her ears.

"I suppose," I ventured, "that you could n't leave me at home, Lucretia?"

"Of course not," replied my sister. "Go out to luncheon alone with two gentlemen! Who ever heard of such a thing?" She gave a final flutter before the glass and turned. "It is a pity your gray linen is so plain," she said; "but wear your cherry ribbons, and you won't look very ugly."

With this consoling remark Lucretia tripped

away, leaving me to rush through my toilet and hasten downstairs with an unbecomingly flushed face and the consciousness of being badly dressed. As I reached the hall, Aunt Jane beckoned me into the dining-room. On the table were a basket of cakes and a tray of tall glasses filled with pink shrub.

"It was the rule your Aunt Caroline sent from Germany," began Aunt Jane in her irrelevant way. "You know these are the little almond biscuit. I want you to carry them in, my face is so red from the oven."

"They will laugh," I said heartlessly; "I am sure they will laugh, Aunt Jane. You know we are going to have luncheon at Mrs. Sparhawk's."

"I do not think it is very nice of her," rejoined Aunt Jane, plaintively, "to try to change everything in Arrowsic. Why should she dine at seven o'clock instead of one? — Will you carry in the tray, Elizabeth, or must I?"

Upon this, of course, I bore the cakes and shrub into the parlor. Ted grinned broadly. Lucretia looked apologetic, and Mr. Hamlin positively aghast. He ate his almond cake, but eyed his shrub dubiously.

" If you detest it," I said softly, with a glance toward Theodore and Lucretia at the piano, — " if you detest it as Father does, and you dare not hurt Aunt Jane's feelings by leaving it, I will pour it out of the window into the flowering currant bush."

He passed me his glass readily.

" I abhor it," he said; and as I emptied the goblet from the window, he bestowed on me a very friendly smile.

The delicacies being now disposed of, we left the house; Lucretia and Theodore walking before, Mr. Hamlin following perforce with me.

" Who are the Sparhawks, anyhow? " asked Mr. Hamlin, rather crossly, striking with his walking-stick at the red thistles which were shiftlessly allowed to grow along the way. "Everywhere I go I hear them quoted, mentioned, and talked about. I saw Mrs. Sparhawk once, but I 've never seen her husband."

"Colonel Sparhawk," I explained, "is an army officer retired on half-pay. I think he has malaria. He wears a single eyeglass, and snaps his cane and tells long stories about the Peninsula. He is always in a great hurry, though he never does anything but begin pictures which he never finishes."

"And Mrs. Sparhawk?"

"Well, Mrs. Sparhawk is either an American who pretends to be English, or an English woman who pretends to be American. I can't tell you about her. She is not like anybody else."

"Is it an archery meeting?"

"Yes, only the whole Club does n't lunch there. Mrs. Sparhawk was telling Lucretia about her colored cook's frozen strawberries, and so she invited us down to taste some, and asked Ted to bring you."

"I did n't want to come," said Mr. Hamlin, ungratefully; "I hate visiting."

"The children are funny," I suggested; "you may like them."

Lucretia turned a reproachful face upon me, and at the same moment I heard a joyous puffing at my side.

"Now, Betty Greenleaf," said Lucretia, elegantly, "you 've gone and brought that dog."

"I did n't bring him," I said, doing my best to look severely at the waggish brown eyes which were raised to mine. "He followed us. He knows he is doing wrong."

"Woof!" said Ned, experimentally, with his eyes fixed on my face, and the suspicion of a wag thrilling his tail.

"Go home!" said Lucretia, in her most judicial manner.

"Go home, sir!" added Theodore, sharply. Ted loves neither my dog nor me.

I added my commands to the others, but, to confess a truth, Ned's strong point is not obedience. He eyed me reproachfully for a moment, then with a sudden leap pretended to regard the whole affair as an enormous joke. He "charged" an instant, made a sudden dash for a wandering bit of paper, shook it violently, then turned his eyes on me, as if he would like to know why I did not laugh. As a matter of course, I did laugh, whereupon Ned considered his point gained, and, quite mad with delight, tumbled over himself repeatedly as he rushed ahead of us down the street.

The Sparhawks live in a very ornate cottage set far back on an untidy lawn. The hedge is ragged, and the stone-paved walk bordered with a wild snarl of syringa bushes and Tartarean honeysuckle. There were once elaborate flower beds, shaped like crescents and diamonds; but neglect has conquered the original intention, and box, striped grass, and a shiftless vine which Harriet calls " creeping Jinny," run riot everywhere.

Doors and windows were all open, and gay Italian awnings fluttered in the slight breeze. Upstairs we heard a shrill voice singing, " Pull for the Shore." Downstairs a piano was being banged upon by some child. From round the corner came a high confusion of cackling fowl, shouting of children, and the regular " clucking " beat of a spoon in a cooking bowl. On the terrace, from which the grass is much worn, as if by the frequent sliding down of children, a gorgeous peacock stood with his tail spread. The front door, though open, was inhospitably barricaded by chairs turned down upon their sides. A scarlet and gray parrot sat meditating upon the balustrade post, and a small black boy lay asleep on the floor, with his funny round head in the full glare of the sunshine.

"There is no bell-knob," said Theodore, looking helplessly about.

"No," replied Lucretia, "it was broken last winter; but there ought to be a dinner-bell about here somewhere. They kept one standing on the piazza for visitors to use."

At the sound of our voices a small black girl, with her wool standing up in a hundred little horns, peeped from the parlor door and fled wildly up the front stairs. Meantime, after some hunting, Ted discovered the bell hidden in the long grass and gave it a vigorous ring. It produced no effect, however, for its sound was drowned entirely, as around the corner of the house came a procession consisting of Rodney Sparhawk, six years old; Bevis, aged four; a Newfoundland dog, and a minute gray kitten. Rodney wore a trailing coat of his father's, and a dangling sword scabbard. He had hung a tin steamer about his neck, upon which he played a deafening tattoo with two iron spoons, and he walked backward, shouting: "Left! Left! I left a good home when I left." His regiment consisted only of Bevis, in exceedingly brief white petticoats, long pink hose, a pair of large brogans, and an old chapeau above his pretty baby face and yellow curls. Bevis appeared to be trumpeter, beside constituting the band, and alternately blew upon a small tin horn and shouted: "Fourther July! Fourther July!" with a volume of voice amazing from so small a person.

At sight of our party the children paused, and a moment of blissful silence ensued. Then Bevis spoke, —

"Tant dit in.   Our tars are in the door. Must n't touch.   Doin' to pay wiz 'em bime by."

With this warning the procession again took up its line of march, joyfully augmented by Ned, uninvited but jovial, and with shouts of "Left! Left!" and "Fourther July!" wound across the lawn, through a gap in the hedge, and disappeared down the street.

In the hush which followed their departure, an unctuous voice came from the direction of the beating spoon, —

" Si, 'got you rule out'n some cook book,' si, 'I'll be boun',' si. 'Jus' wish ye could oncet eat a *rale* chick'n patty. Some o' my puff paste and chick'n done up in cream,' si; 'I believe ye'd be a better Chris'n ef ye could jus' *taste* one o' my chick'n patties,' si. Thar, 'clar for 't, Mis' Sparrock, I's jus' that free with her, I was *so !*"

Laughter followed, — a lady-like ripple and an oily, rich chuckle, — in the midst of which Theodore again rang the dinner-bell.

" I suppose that is the children," a clear voice said, " but you might just look, Aunt Judy."

At this a shining black face, under a gay plaid turban, looked from a door at the end of the hall.

" ' Clar for 't ! " exclaimed the owner, coming briskly forward, with a jovial smile of welcome which displayed her beautiful white teeth, " ef 't aint Miss Greenleaf! Tought 't was likely dem no-'count chil'n. Dere allus ringin' de bal."

She cleared away the chairs, and touched the sleeping black boy on the rug with her foot.

" You, Sam," she said easily, " come off dat flo', and go 'long 'bout you business. Don' yer stay yere no mo' whar yer don' b'long at. D'yer min'?"

The boy, at her thrust, curled up like a touch-me-not, and rolled softly away under the stairs, while the old woman showed us into the parlor and disappeared.

It was a long room, this parlor; indeed, there were two rooms, divided by a curtain of faded red velvet, and the polished, bare floors were strewn with rugs of dull, soft tints. This was a scandal to most of the good Arrowsic matrons, who believed it better to dispense with a parlor entirely, unless one was able to carpet it. The four windows were wide open, and the lace draperies hung outside as if somebody had intended to prepare the room for sweeping, and abandoned the idea. On the centre-table was a shallow bowl full of exquisite violets, a riding whip, a pair of soiled white gauntlets, an open copy of " Sintram " in the original, a sponge, and a bonbonnière in the form of a silver slipper. There were fine etchings on the sage-tinted walls; and everywhere, on chairs, tables, ottomans, and all about the floor, leaning against the walls and the chair-legs, were the Colonel's paintings in fifty stages of incompletion. A palette occupied the piano-stool; the piano was decorated with writing materials and half-emptied wine-glasses; and on the hearth a small monkey sat, eating cake and watching us with his little bright eyes.

Hardly a seat was unoccupied by books, fans, or embroidery, so we stood about rather stupidly.

Lucretia tried to look politely unconscious, and frowned terribly at Theodore, who was openly entertained. Mr. Hamlin stood by a window, and examined with much interest the name of the man who sold him his straw hat. After a season of silence, a voice called from an upstairs window, —

"*Did* anybody come, Aunt Judy? Here I am, if you are looking for me."

Upon this, Aunt Judy issued from the carriage house, crossed the lawn, came in the front door, and puffed noisily upstairs.

"'Clar for 't!'" she exclaimed, "done been ebberywhar to fine yer. Ben all tro' de house an' de barns an' de garding. Rosalby, she's done gone to hunt ye in de strawb'ry bed, an' Sam, he's done gone out to de hen-house. Whar ye been hid to?"

"Why, I ran up the other stairs," was the reply.

After this followed whisperings, some suppressed laughter, and a good deal of running to and fro. There was calling for "Almira," and "little black Sam;" there was a crash of breaking china, and the excited barking of a dog. After some time, Mrs. Sparhawk's voice exclaimed, —

"Good heavens! Then I must have left it downstairs. Run, Rosalba, and get it somehow, before any of them see it. What? Why, so it is. How stupid!"

After this came a short silence, then the swish of skirts on the bare oak stairs, and in came Mrs. Sparhawk, perfectly dressed, perfectly cordial, perfectly at her ease, and apparently sublimely unconscious of the noisy house, the untidy rooms, or the length of time she had kept us waiting.

"How simply angelic of you all to come and see me this morning!" she exclaimed cordially. "I have been absolutely dying of ennui. I told the Colonel that if this direful stupidity continued we should really have to be divorced for the sake of variety. Three years I was at Tehuantepec, Mr. Hamlin, and positively it was not so dull as Arrowsic. There, at least, the natives were forever killing one another, and one was always on the *qui vive* against centipedes."

Lucretia's formal, polite little greeting was quite lost in this flow of words; and Theodore and Mr. Hamlin and I grinned inanely, and did not attempt to speak.

"The Colonel and I endured each other quite as long as we could," continued Mrs. Sparhawk, airily, "and then he went down to sketch the intervale meadows, and I was driven to gossip with Aunt Judy. Do sit down, if you can find enough empty chairs. Aunt Judy ought really to have sent Rosalba in to set things to rights. I dare say she may have done so, but the child will always play on the piano instead of dusting — not that I

blame her. I'd do the same myself, I'm
sure."

Our hostess laughed cheerfully, put up her
eyeglass, which was always falling down, and
swept across the room, knocking over several
pictures and an Indian jug with her train. She
tilted up a low arm-chair and emptied it of a
tiny Spanish poodle who had entered the room
with her.

"Cherubino," she said, "you are a nasty, selfish creature; did you know it, little beast?"

She sank into the velvet depths and continued
talking easily.

"Is it not strange that a dog will be so
intensely selfish? You may trust Cherubino
always to secure this chair for his nap, — quite
the softest and easiest chair in the whole house,
I assure you, — and yet this little pig will calmly
take it without a thought that another might
enjoy it as well as he. Ah, well! One must
take them as they are created. I suppose one

can't expect to find dogs with the finer feelings
of human beings, can one, Mr. Hamlin?"

By this time we had all succeeded in finding
seats, and Lucretia and I had become shame-
faced under the awful conviction that Mrs. Sparhawk had entirely forgotten that she had ever
invited us to come to luncheon. The injured
Cherubino was being forced to beg for chocolates from the silver slipper, which he did
sulkily and without enthusiasm. Suddenly Mrs.
Sparhawk turned.

"You have come to luncheon," she said,
laughing. "Now do not think I entirely forgot
it, for that is not so; but I talk so much that
you might think me volatile. The Colonel was
speaking of your coming at the breakfast table
this morning, — positively, — and Aunt Judy is
making chicken pâté. Cherubino, you rascal,
don't stand so one-sided! I declare, though,
I *had* forgotten that the Archery Club met here
this afternoon! I do hope they 'll remember to

fetch a target. The children have quite destroyed ours, little vandals."

She boxed Cherubino's ears lightly, and leaning back in the chair, put on her glasses and settled her white gown.

" I abominate archery," she declared. " It murders one's wrist in such a manner, and then, one never can hit the nasty target, one must stand so far away; beside, does n't it strike you, Mr. Hamlin, that they use very small targets in Arrowsic?"

" Minute," agreed Mr. Hamlin, seriously. " However, I think Miss Dudley and young Greenleaf would hit in any case; and if you will all pardon me, I should say the rest of the Club would miss a target as large as a cart-wheel."

" It *is* a nasty club," assented Mrs. Sparhawk. " By the bye, Mr. Hamlin, I wonder of whom you constantly remind me. I should say it was somebody in China. I spent ten mortal years

in China, and your face somehow reminds me
of Hong-Kong."

Somebody once added up the years that Mrs.
Sparhawk had spent in various spots on the
globe, and found that, according to her own
confession, she must at present be between
eighty-five and ninety years of age.

"I have never been in China," began Mr.
Hamlin, with that feeling of vague foolishness
one always has when one's face is remarked
upon, when steps sounded on the piazza, and
Colonel Sparhawk, with his easel, tin color-box,
and white umbrella, came into the room.

He is a man of middle height, inclining
strongly to stoutness, of a florid complexion
and pompous bearing, but with a very affable
manner, a leaning toward gallantry, and a deep
voice, rather husky from good living, — the
last person one would select for an invalid;
yet his retirement was due to malarial fevers,
and he is popularly said to be dogged by a

gaunt and chilly bogy who only waits a bad season or the like opportunity to pounce upon him.

" This is delightful," he declared, as he greeted us; " a charming surprise. After all, surprises are the spice of life."

Mrs. Sparhawk laughed and adjusted her eyeglass.

" Now, my life," she said, " do not pretend that we were not speaking of the pleasure at breakfast, because you *know* we *were!* "

" True, very true," briskly rejoined the Colonel; " most assuredly, herzliebchen, but I 'm sure the young ladies will pardon the mistake of an old soldier. I remember that one morning when we were on the Isthmus, it was intensely warm, not a breath stirring, and some of the natives had — "

" Not now, my own darling," interrupted Mrs. Sparhawk, rising; " it just occurs to me that I have been horribly remiss. These young ladies have had no chance to lay aside their hats and gloves. Really, liebchen, I shall throttle that wretched monkey of yours if he continues to glare at me in that offensive manner. He is uncommonly nasty to-day."

" Always as you say, my own," said the Colonel, as he gallantly held the door open for us to pass out.

Mrs. Sparhawk deposited us in a big, sunny, untidy chamber, where she left us with the information that we should find the rouge in the upper bureau drawer. Lucretia turned upon me with a horrified face.

"She thinks we paint!" she exclaimed; "and she never expected us to luncheon. She had forgotten all about it."

" She got over it nicely."

" I had the greatest mind to go home," said Lucretia, tragically; "only I did n't know what to say, and I was afraid of making a bad matter worse."

" Pooh ! " I replied unconcernedly, " why should you care? She does n't. I don't mind a bit."

" You are always getting into fixes," retorted my sister, severely. " You are used to them, and I am not. Where is the towel?"

There was none to be found, but this was a trifle; and where one had ivory-backed brushes, pink Sevres boxes, gold-topped perfume flasks, and satin pincushions, how could one grumble at an empty ewer, no pins, and a total lack of towels?

In the parlor we found Rodney and Bevis. The regiment was disbanded, and they were playing with the monkey and partaking of rations of seed-cakes, of which they had a wonderful supply.

" Bevis, my man," said the Colonel, who adored his children, " come here and speak to these charming young ladies. Let them see you give the officers' salute."

But alas for pretty Bevis! He proved upon closer inspection to be both dirty and tousled. His yellow curls were in wild confusion, there was a horrible blue bruise above one eye, and a red gash on his left cheek.

"Why, Bevis!" exclaimed the Colonel, with solicitude, "you have hurt yourself badly. You are a brave little man not to cry, but how did it happen? Tell papa. My life, pardon me, but will you look at Bevis?"

Mrs. Sparhawk was talking with Theodore about Morris wall papers. She put up her glasses and regarded Bevis for an instant with a bored expression. She gave a little French shrug.

"I see nothing the matter," she said, "except that his face is unconscionably dirty. You may be quite certain, *mon ami*, that he would cry if he were hurt. I never knew him to restrain himself from mere motives of delicacy."

" Pooh ! " sneered Rodney, somewhat envious of the sensation that Bevis was making. " He is n't hurted any 't all. He 's only a ninjun; he painted hisself out o' the little silver tubes upstairs."

" But you look shockingly," declared the Colonel. " I am really mortified that these nice young ladies should see you. Come with me, both of you. We must go at once and find Almira;" and the gallant Colonel led his dishevelled sons away.

Mrs. Sparhawk watched their departure with the dispassionate mien of one having no manner of personal interest in the affair.

"The poor Colonel," she said. "What a bother children are, to be sure! Did it ever occur to you, Mr. Hamlin, that they are like teeth? They begin to make trouble as soon as they enter the world, and one is always tormented by them until one is rid of them." She opened and closed her fan, and then added

swiftly: "Now do not think I am so inhuman
as to mean until they die; of course I mean
until they are married."

At this moment the little black boy announced that luncheon was ready, and Colonel
Sparhawk joined us.

The luncheon was quite as incongruous as
everything else in that singular household.
Delicate gold and lilac china and old India ware
were side by side with bits of ironstone. The
linen, though torn, was richly embroidered.
There was an epergne of Sevres where lovely
rosy cupids rioted among lilies and ferns. The
Colonel barbecued thin slices of ham upon a
silver blazer, the chicken pâtés were served in
tin dishes, the coffee pot had no handles and
very little nose. The cookery, however, was
marvellous. Not Harriet's choicest triumphs,
nor the most secret of Aunt Jane's ancestral
receipts, could equal that delicacy of seasoning,
those fine and mysterious flavors, that exquisite

and melting "turn" to which each dish was brought.

About midway of the meal the door was pushed open by Bevis, angelic in white and azure, his curls like spun gold, and his rosy little face cleared of its war paint.

"Comin' to eat wid you," he announced winsomely.

"Oh, no, you are not," replied his father. "You will have your bread and milk as usual in the nursery."

A small cloud crossed the placid heaven of Bevis's face.

"Bread an' milt is nasty," urged he, sweetly; "Bevis wants storbies, lots o' storbies, an' cakes an' tarts."

"Go away, Bevis," said the Colonel, briefly.

"Don't want to g'way," smiled Bevis; "want to come in an' eat wid you."

"Bevis," demanded his father, "do you wish me to take you to Almira?"

Apparently Bevis did not, for he at once began a hasty retreat, and catching his foot in a rug, fell to the floor, where he lay howling lustily. Instantly Mrs. Sparhawk looked up from her strawberries and put down the sugar sifter. She rose from the table and swept tempest-like across the room to clasp the wailing Bevis in her arms. The Colonel became conscience-stricken.

"My own love," said he, "has he really hurt himself? What ails him ?"

She turned and faced her husband with the air of a tragedy queen, her head thrown back and the child close to her shoulder.

"Oh, nothing, Colonel Sparhawk," she exclaimed vehemently; "a mere trifle, too light to be even spoken of. Pray go on with your luncheon. My child has fallen and killed himself. He is dying; that is all. I see plainly that it is not of the slightest consequence to you."

The Colonel looked half amused and half distressed.

"I want to be to de tabul," sobbed the dying Bevis.

"And so you shall, my liebling," said his mother.

She established him at her side, and smoothed out the peach-colored satin ribbons at her belt. No May morning was ever blander than her unruffled face.

"Now, why is it," smilingly demanded she, regarding Mr. Hamlin over the blue jar of Chinese sweetmeats she began serving, — "why is it that these cumquots remind me of you, just as Hong-Kong seems to do?"

"My heart," ventured the Colonel, "how irrelevant you sometimes are!"

"Limkin!" exclaimed his wife, reproachfully.

"Limkin," the form into which the black cook had corrupted *liebchen,* is one of Mrs. Sparhawk's many names for the Colonel.

"Well, but are you not?" pursued the Colonel, playfully.

"I don't suppose, limkin," said Mrs. Sparhawk, much aggrieved, "that you have the slightest idea how much fault you find with me."

"My life," exclaimed the conscience-stricken Colonel, "to find a fault in you would be impossible."

"Then I wish you would not appear to do so," pouted Mrs. Sparhawk.

"My own love," protested the Colonel, "on my honor I never will again."

Matters being thus adjusted, Mrs. Sparhawk went on serving the cumquots with a pair of curious silver tongs, while Bevis beside her revelled in berries and cream, as absolutely forgotten by his mother as if he had slept for ages in an Egyptian catacomb.

Very soon another step, Rodney's this time, was heard in the hall, and Rodney's head was thrust in at the door.

"I want to be to the table too," he said.

"You cannot come, you untidy child," said his mother, eying him with strong disfavor.

"But you let Bevis," urged Rodney, with vague ideas of justice seething in his childish brain.

"Bevis is clean and lovely, and you are a nasty little gypsy," said Mrs. Sparhawk. "Go away at once, or I will tell Joe to run the lawn-mower over you."

"If you do," replied the undaunted Rodney, by no means behind his mother in the invention of direful threats, — "if you do I will turn into a bear and chew off your head and all your fingers. Then how'll you feel?"

At this moment the black woman came in with the ices.

"Don' yer min', honey," she said, with unctuous sympathy; "jes' you come long o' you ole Aunt Judy an' see wat she done made yer."

The fickle mind of Rodney being thus diverted, he clattered briskly across the room and disappeared.

"Really," laughed Mrs. Sparhawk, "I never saw the equal of Aunt Judy. She has been with me ever since Rodney was a baby, and she is a faithful soul, but the way she spoils those children is abominable. If she says no, she does not mean no, and of course the boys are aware of it. She has n't a shadow of firmness, not a shadow. No, Bevis, not another berry to-day, not one."

"I had seven, five, free," pleaded Bevis, plaintively. "I want a hunnerd."

"You have had already more than five hundred, you little gourmand."

"Peese, peese!" said Bevis, holding out his plate with both hands.

"Bevis," demanded his mother, "when I say no, do I mean it?"

"No," replied Bevis, boldly; "you say no,

and den you say ' don't boover,' and den I go an' do it."

Mrs. Sparhawk laughed heartily.

" What will that child say next ? " she asked. " Colonel, do give him some berries; he certainly deserves them."

" When I lived in Baltimore," began Mr. Hamlin, joining in the laugh, " I used to know a — "

" Baltimore," interrupted Mrs. Sparhawk. " There! I know all about it now. Hong-Kong and the cumquots and everything. It is that Judge Hamlin. Limkin, don't you remember that Judge Hamlin we met in Hong-Kong? He was going round the world for his health, or else he had ruined his health in going round the world; anyhow, he afterward wrote a book on ' Eastern Jurisdiction,' and he lives in Baltimore. Do you know him, Mr. Hamlin ? "

"He is my uncle," replied Mr. Hamlin, quietly.

Mrs. Sparhawk put on her glasses and regarded the young man with a new interest.

"You look like him," she said; "it is not the name only which made me think of him. We owe you even more than the hospitality due to the ordinary visitor to Arrowsic. Your uncle entertained us many times in his beautiful home in Baltimore."

She was rising from the table as she spoke. The earliest of the archery arrivals was announced, and she can hardly have caught the reply of Mr. Hamlin, —

"I shall be quite content to waive any honors given me on my uncle's account. My own dues as Mr. Foster's friend will content me," he said rather stiffly.

VI.

WHAT BOB SAYS.

THE other day at Mrs. Sparhawk's — I mean when our Archery Club met there — we made a jolly old plan, if we can only put it through.

Our Archery Club is a queer affair anyway; and I did n't much blame Hamlin for laughing, for some of the girls do shoot worse than words can tell. Josephine Foster is so afraid of snapping her wrist that she acts like a perfect muff; and Lucretia is rather afraid of her hands, too, though she shoots exactly according to rules, as she does everything else. Betty never hits the target, though I never can just tell why, and she always loses her arrows. Emily Dudley is the only girl who is much good at shooting, and the men are not so much better than the women. As for me, I can hit the gold often enough; but I never get any credit for it, because I don't hold my bow according to rule. Mr. Harris says he would rather hold his bow correctly and never hit the target, than to hit the gold and hold his bow as I do.

Well, that afternoon, you know, we seemed to be shooting rather worse than usual; and somebody — Hamlin, I think it was — happened to say that it would be a bad look for us if we had nothing to eat except what we could shoot. Then some one else said that we could shoot things enough if we were only off in the woods; and then Ted Foster said that we might try the plan when we went up to Sippican.

We have a Sippican party every season, and sometimes we camp out for a whole month. We have big water-proof tents, and we build a stone fireplace. We find perch and blueberries on the mountain as big as grapes — at least, of course, I mean the perch are in the pond.

Sippican is the Indian name for Clear Water; and there's a pond and a mountain, and it's the completest place to camp out in that you ever saw. You have no end of fun up there. Sometimes it rains, and the tents leak, and the fire won't burn, and you pretend you are cast away on a desert island; and you play all sorts of pranks, and go trouting up the brook, and have tableaux and tell stories in the evenings; and the days are so short, and Lucretia is shocked because you eat so much, and everything is just as jolly as it can be.

So this year we're going to try the new plan. Of course it all began in fun, but most everybody has agreed to it, and it will be fun enough. Aunt Jane is sure we shall starve; but Fred Harris and I are sure that we can shoot squirrels and quail and partridges enough for the whole party — there aren't any game laws at Sippican. There used to be bears up there, but I don't suppose you could scare one up now.   I'd just like to meet a bear, though! Would n't I just send an arrow *ping* through his heart, and we'd have bear-steaks for supper at Camp Sippican!

I was almost afraid that Father would n't let me go, because I'm studying for the fall examinations; but Aunt Jane luckily took it into her head that I looked pale — though I know it was only because the green blinds were shut — and Betty put in a good word for me.   So Father has given in, and I'm going; and if we don't just have a famous time, then my name is not Bob Greenleaf!

VII.

WHAT BETTY SAYS.

"THE shay is ready," said Harriet, " and the young man is waitin'."

She folded her arms severely, and stood watching me with the disapproving air which seems to be the special attribute of old house-keeper-domestics who have known one from childhood.

" No need to prink yourself out any great," she remarked rather caustically; " you won't meet nobody but cattle, and as for the young man, I don't think he's one of the sort to take notice."

I made no direct reply, for whether Mr. John Hamlin " took notice " or not was of far less consequence to me than the fact that Bob had basely turned me over to a stranger, simply because he wanted to go off on one of his innumerable fishing excursions with Fred Harris.

"And for my part," continued Harriet, "if it was necessary for your par to go flighting off to Portland, it seems 'f you need n't go rampaging about the country with strange young men."

"That's Bob's fault," I returned, picking up my gloves. "Father expected him to go; and as for Mr. Hamlin, I'm sure it's kind of him to be willing to drive me about with the medicines that Father must send."

"Probably you 'll get 'em all mixed higgledy-piggledy with your talkin'," sniffed Harriet, following me down the shallow old stairs; but she was prevented from uttering further forebodings by reaching the open door, just outside which was Judge Peters's loose-jointed ramshackle chaise, drawn by the gaunt old sorrel mare, "Jane Savage."

Mr. Hamlin with cheerful alacrity helped me to a seat.

"Now we 'll see how a civil engineer can run a medical expedition," he said. "Are we all ready?"

We were, but apparently Jane Savage was not. She was deeply engaged in gazing at Harriet, who had just made a tumultuous appearance at the door, — a vision of long, waving arms and nodding feather duster. She looked like a fury, but she was only expelling the flies which had feloniously entered. As soon as the green door was closed, Jane Savage started of her own free will, and taking her own pace, presently left the village behind her.

At the foot of the hill a shallow, stony brook crosses the road, and just beyond, nestling in a little valley, is the group of poor houses known as "Hungry Hollow."

"You know," announced Mr. Hamlin, "that I depend upon you to direct me to the houses, and to do the talking; I am only the parcel delivery."

"Very well," I replied; "first of all, then, we stop at the third house on the right."

It was a dismal, dreary little house, standing close upon the dusty road, and staring blankly at us from shutterless windows. A barn much larger than the house stood just across the road. Everybody seemed to be away or asleep, except a child who was sitting on the sunken door-step with her elbows on her knees, and her sharp little chin in her hands. She was a most aged and unchildish-looking child, with hair bleached by the sun, and small blue eyes which looked oddly light-colored when contrasted with her tiny weather-beaten face. As we stopped, she looked up dully, then let her eyes fall, and resumed her occupation of scraping the warm sand back and forth with her bare feet.

"Isabel," I cried, "here is Eliza's sleeping

draught. Father had to go to Portland to-day, but he will come over to-morrow."

The child neither raised her head nor stopped moving her feet through the sand.

" Lizy don't want no med'sin," she said; "she wants some flowers."

" Some flowers?" I queried.

" I said flowers," said Isabel, rather sharply. " Did n't ye hear?"

" You must not be so cross, Isabel," I said. " If Eliza wants some flowers, I 'll send her a bunch to-morrow."

" She don't want a bunch," said Isabel; " she wants a cross an' a wreath. She 's goin' to hev a funril day after to-morrer, Lizy is, an' she wants a wreath an' a cross like what Emma Parker had to hern."

Shocked and quieted, we hesitated for something to say; and, as I looked about, Isabel's mother appeared from somewhere down the road. She is curiously like Isabel, though tall

and gaunt. Her hard, brown face under her
gingham bonnet worked and twisted a little as
she saw me, but she blinked her eyes and
closed her lips in a reliant, repressive way.
Her large-jointed, labor-stained hands clasped
and unclasped nervously.

"Yes," she said, "she's gone, Lizy is. You
can tell yer par she went easy; dropped off to
sleep and never woke up."   .

She stopped a moment to swallow a lump in
her throat, then she went on dully, —

"Might ez wal die, I s'pose, an' done with it,
ez go pindlin' along an' sufferin'. No great use
in livin', fur as I see. Lizy, she's the seventh
I've buried. Live to fifteen or sixteen, then
grow peaked an' fade away an' die. Don't
seem to be no real reason why they should
ever been born."

"Mrs. Hathaway," I cried, "don't talk in this
way; you must not. Is there nothing I can do
to help you?"

"No," she replied in her stiff, practical way, "there aint nothin' to do. The neighbors hev been in to do for us, an' he has writ a postal to tell her Uncle Silas an' Aunt Laviny to come down to the funril."

Isabel on the door-step had raised her head.

"But we aint got no flowers," she said, with dull persistence.

"You shall have all you want, Isabel," I said. "I will send you a basket early to-morrow morning."

The child's weird, elf-like face lighted up with a look of positive pleasure; but it was her mother who spoke.

"I'm sure, I'm 'bleeged to ye," she said; "you mean kind, I know. Lizy she always talked a terrible sight about what a beautiful funril Emma Parker hed. It was pooty, too. I'm sure you're very 'bleegin'."

With a stiff nod by way of farewell, she went around the house. In silence Isabel followed

6

her, and in silence too we rode on up the rise
and out of Hungry Hollow with its poverty and
sorrow and loss.

The landscape changed from sad to beautiful as we went on. Peace and plenty smiled
in the broad patches of corn-land where the
wind rustled the fresh, green ribbons and the
silk already burst from the close, sweet husks.
There were wide hay-fields too, where the second growth of grass was exquisite with tints of
amethyst and dull yellow, and dashes of red
sorrel.

" Do we stop at the next house ? " my companion asked at last.

"Not the white one," I answered, "the big
yellow one on the hill. We have to let down
the bars. This is the Tuell farm."

The bars being properly lowered, my companion led Jane Savage up the rocky ascend-
ing pasture which formed the lawn of the Tuell
place.

"Hand me the pills and potions," said the young man, cheerfully, "and I will carry them in."

"You had better go round to the back door," I mildly suggested.

"No, I shall not," he said stoutly; "I shall give them one chance to open the sacred front door."

He went up confidently through tansy and "old-maids" to the green-painted door. There was a fanlight above it, and a very good old brass knocker, with which Mr. Hamlin proceeded to wake the echoes within the house. There was no response; and for some seconds we waited, studying the wreaths of gay flowers upon the green paper curtains of the parlor windows, and the pair of conch-shells — a gift of some seafaring relative — which adorn the little niches formed by the side-lights. The bees hummed drowsily among the hollyhocks, and from afar came the long-drawn "kark,

kark, kar-ar-ark," of some unseen barn-yard
fowl.

"It ·is no use, you see," I said triumphantly;
"you must try the other door."

The young man was persistent. He knocked
again. No sound but the hen and the bees.
Then he grew impatient and knocked clamor-
ously. Then at length a step was heard within,
and a sharp voice exclaimed, —

"Don't knock the door down. You 'll have to
go round the back way; this door don't open."

Mr. Hamlin refused to be properly humili-
ated. He cast a stony glance at me, and proceeded to the back door. This opened directly,
and a small, alert woman appeared. She had
a pinched, acid little face, and with her neat
cotton gown and closely pinned hair, had the
air of being clewed up, so to speak, against any
tempest of life.

"Wal?" she said with some asperity and a
rising accent.

"I brought some medicine from Dr. Green-leaf," said Mr. Hamlin, apologetically, and added an account of the circumstances which prevented Father from coming himself.

Mrs. Tuell took the bottle and examined the label with some suspicion.

"What is your name?" she demanded, "and who's that settin' in the shay?"

"My name is Hamlin," said the young man, quite meekly, "and it is the Doctor's daughter, Miss Greenleaf, with me."

"Oh," said Mrs. Tuell, half appeased, "'t is, is it? Wal, doctor *sent* the drops?"

"Yes," more meekly than ever.

"Betty," she called, raising her voice to address me, "tell yer par that the baby's come out wal with the red goom. Cathrine she's worried about it, but I tell her all strong children hev it. You tell yer par."

With this she abruptly darted into the house, banging the door energetically behind her, but as we were turning the carriage about she reopened the door.

" Be sure ye put the bars up," she cried, " or Durgin's sheep will be trapesin' in."

She once more vanished, and we rolled slowly down the slope to the road, not forgetting to put up the bars.

"What a truly horrible woman ! " exclaimed Mr. Hamlin, devoutly, as we once more jogged upon our way. " Is her husband dead ? "

" Oh, no," I answered, " did n't you see him peeping out from behind the wood-house? He is a very good man, and so afraid of his wife that he dares not call his soul his own."

" I don't wonder," said Mr. Hamlin, fervently.

He seemed really to be quite depressed, as though he still felt Mrs. Tuell's snapping eyes upon him. He became so noticeably lax in his hold on the reins that Jane Savage decided to try a little browsing, and turned suggestively toward the ditch. Recalled by a sudden tightening of the rein, she threw a reproachful glance over her left shoulder and walked on with an air of meek but injured dignity.

The old chaise swayed from side to side and creaked drowsily. Little white and yellow butterflies hovered over the mullen and white yarrow. Where the sandy road was hottest the cicadas were uttering their seething song, and now and again we passed the hay-fields, where the mowers stopped work to look at us, and wiped their scythes on wisps of freshly cut grass. It was past eleven o'clock when we stopped at the home of Deacon Asa Jewett, whose daughter Lucilla was bed-ridden and helpless from a spinal trouble. The Jewett house was a red painted cottage with large low chimneys and an ample, rambling wing. There was no front yard. An ancient lilac-tree grew on either side of the door. On the left side was the kitchen garden; on the right a shady old orchard with a row of bee-hives on a

wooden bench. A great butternut-tree shaded
the house on the orchard end. A rusty tea-
kettle hung with apparent irrelevance to one
of its lower branches, but the cord attached to
it explained its connection with the grindstone
standing below. Outside the wall, but still in
the grateful shade of the butternut, an old man
was sitting on a chair which had lost its back.
He was whittling, but he stopped as we drew
up, and without speaking gazed at us with
lack-lustre blue eyes.

"I have brought Lucilla's plasters, Deacon
Jewett," I said, as I stepped unassisted from the
low chaise. "I have some magazines for her;
shall I go right in?"

"Yas, yas," said the old man, rising and
coming forward. "I see now it's the doctor's
gel. Hardly knowed ye jest at first. Ye haint
ben round so frequent with doctor as ye used
ter. Who's that with ye in the shay?"

"It is Mr. Hamlin, from Baltimore. He is

visiting at the Fosters'," I answered. " I will run in myself with these things, shall I ? "

As I made my way to the side door a hoarse voice said suddenly, " O Lord! Lord! Lord! " and then immediately broke into a peal of discordant laughter. It was Mrs. Jewett's parrot, a disreputable old bird who could swear many a broad, mouth-filling oath in Spanish, but was forced, by ignorance, to be almost respectable in English. Like Mrs. Tuell's conch-shells, the parrot was a sign that we were not far inland after all.

" I'm proper glad to see ye," said Mrs. Jewett, appearing from the kitchen. " You come right into Lucilla's room. She is so glad to see a bit of comp'ny."

Lucilla was lying on a feather-bed, under a " rising-sun " bed-quilt which was a dream of horrors in itself. The green paper curtains were pulled up awry, and no window was open, though Mrs. Jewett was a tender mother and tried to make the invalid comfortable according to her lights.

"She's ben expectin' of your par all the mornin'," Mrs. Jewett went on, with an affectionate pat to the rising-sun quilt. "I do declare she has nigh about wore me out, Lucilla has, worryin' me to look out o' winder every minute to see if doctor warn't comin'."

At this I repeated the story of Father's having been called to Portland, and I only escaped a severe cross-questioning about Mr. Hamlin by presenting the magazines and a little parcel of light work.

"Law, now," exclaimed Mrs. Jewett, admiringly, "do jest look at the silk pieces that she's picked up for ye! See this now, aint it turky-ish, though! I warrant now ye'll want to be bolstered right up, as soon as ye've hed your broth, and begin to set your new quilt this very day."

As I went out of the house, I saw Deacon

Jewett standing with one foot on the hub of a wheel of the chaise. He was chewing a straw and looking alternately at Mr. Hamlin and down at his foot.

"I wish ye hed time," he was saying, "to step over with me an' jest take a look at it. I cal'lated to hev that lot preambulated this summer, come what might."

"It would do you no good," returned Mr. Hamlin, "for me to go down and look at the land. I should have to see the deeds."

"Wal, now," said the deacon, slowly, "I tell ye jest how 't was. It was this way: I went over to see old Squar Bisbee, him as married Woodman Puslifer's third darter, Lowizy, and says I to him, 'Squar,' says I, 'this ere lot hez got to be preambulated,' says I, 'no two ways about it. Ef it haint,' says I, 'an' ef it can't be done peaceable, why, all is, Lyman Dunlap and me 'll hev to go to law about it,' says I. Wal, the squar he said that he never sot up to know nothin' about surveyin', but he 'd studied on it a spell when he was to Litchfield Academy, an' he hed a compass thet belonged to his father, old Squar Lemuel Bisbee, and so I says — "

" Laws, Asa," interrupted Mrs. Jewett, who had followed me out to the garden, and set briskly to gathering beans, " don't you bother the gentleman about that old story. Once get you a talkin' about your land tribulations an' you never have no idea where to stop."

" I sh'd git through a considerable spell sooner, Silviny," said the deacon, drily, " ef I 's allowed to say my say."

" Well, go on," said Mr. Hamlin, biting his mustache.

" *Madre! Madre! Madre!* " cackled the parrot, who had come to join in the conversation, and was standing on the garden fence.

" Shet up, ye tarnal critter ! " said the old man, sharply, to which the bird responded, " Lord ! Lord ! Lord ! " and burst into a hoarse laugh.

"Wal," resumed the deacon, "as I was sayin',
I went over to the squar's and says I to him,
'Squar,' says I, 'that lot hes got to be preambulated fust or last,' says I, 'or Lyman Dunlap an' me, we'll hev — '"

"Law, father, you've said all that once a'
ready," said Mrs. Jewett, briskly.

"Ef you can explain this marter better than
what I can, Mis' Jewett," said the deacon, with
dignity, "I sh'd be proud to hev ye do it."

"Oh, I don't pretend to it, father," replied
his wife, "I don't pretend to it. Only don't
go so fur round Robin Hood's barn, that 's all
I meant."

"Wal," resumed the old man once more, "I
went over to Squar Bisbee an' says I, 'This ere
lot hes got to be preambulated,' says I, 'or
Lyman Dunlap an' me 'll hev to go to law.' So
the squar he fetched his compass an' chain
over one mornin' an' we got out a copy of the
deeds, an' then we went down to the parster — "

" Mother! come to supper!" interrupted the parrot. "O *Madre! Madre!* —"

" Shet up your tarnal squawkin'," said the deacon, making a mock start toward the bird, who immediately fell into extravagant peals of hoarse laughter, and stepped off sideways along the fence toward a black-cherry tree.

" So the squar he fetched over his compass an' chain one mornin' an' we went down to the parster. The squar he sighted 'round a spell, and says he, 'We'll take the gable winder of Widder Thayer's house and run direct to that,' says he. So he started and kep along pretty free till all to once he come butt agin that big rock-maple ye can jest see the top of. So there the squar he sot off a few feet to the northered, an' then kep on an' got Lias down to help him and run a tol'able straight line nigh to the middle of the eend of old Lyman Dunlap's sheep parster. Then old Lyme he come out, mad's a hopper, an' his son Chapman with him, — the

one that went off to Arizony arterwards, an'
got to be postmaster somewheres out there, an'
died, — an' old Lyme he fetched along another
deed, an' says he, 'You'll get yourselves intc
trouble,' says he, 'ef you keep on in this ere
direction, now I warn ye.' So the squar, bein'
a peaceable man, an' not likin' to make no fuss,
and I bein' gone up to the house at the time to
fetch a hatchet, he sot back a matter o' two
yards on tother side. Then Lias he follered it
out alone a spell, while squar, bein' a very
commodatin' man, went up to help Chapman
Dunlap git a turnip out'n a cow's throat. So I
says then to Lias, 'Now, Lias,' says I —"

Just here a small horn was blown within the
house, and Mrs. Jewett's warm, red face was
turned triumphantly from the bean vines.

"There now, father," she said, "you'll *hev* to
stop and let the gentleman alone. That's Lucilla's horn, and it means that she wants her
par. She blows a horn for him, and rings a bell

for me. Now, father, you know you never keep Lucilla waitin'."

" Wal, wal," said the deacon, reluctantly, " wal, wal, I s'pose so. I 'll see ye when ye come back along, and then mebbe ye 'll step down an' take a look at the lot."

" Perhaps," replied the young man; and he gave a sudden jerk to the reins which caused Jane Savage to start down the hill at a most unusual pace.

"What a tedious old numskull," laughed Mr. Hamlin.

"Well," I rejoined severely, "you ought to have known better than to let him know your profession."

" But he asked me."

"Of course he asked you; but if you are going to tell these people all they ask you, you will have to reveal all your deadliest secrets. Deacon Jewett is nearly crazy with land quarrels."

" We will go home by some other way," said

the young man, decidedly; " I do not dare to risk a second meeting with the deacon to-day."

" We shall be longer getting home," I objected, "and it is nearly dinner time."

" If you are hungry you shall have some raspberries," he replied; " but I shall absolutely *not* risk Deacon Jewett again to-day."

Our way lay through lower and moister lands now. We crossed a brook full of brown stones, dark basins, and sunny shallows. At our left, in the marshy meadow, the stream widened into a placid pool. Blue pickerel-weed and yellow beaver lilies grew here, and above them darted the burnished dragon-flies, swift yet aimless. Over the walls clambered the wild convolvulus, with large pink-and-white bells. The wild honeysuckle, white and frail, filled the warm air with its heavy fragrance. There is so much sweetness in these low-lying meadows that it was a real joy to come once more to higher land; to drive through a delicious bit of beech-

wood, where the scarlet fire-lilies flamed in the
hollows among the sturdy brakes.   It was just
beyond the cool and pretty beech-wood that we
came to the old Butterfield house, our next and
last stopping-place.

There was no need here of alighting to let
down the bars, for they were already down, and
some cows and sheep were cropping the sorrel,
thistles, and " poverty weed " which formed the
chief part of the herbage.   The house is of two
stories, square and unpainted.   Its building was
evidently begun by somebody whose ambition
outran his wealth; for all the upper windows
were boarded up, and the front door, lacking
the usual flight of steps, had the appearance of
having been left stranded by some high tide,
half-way up the front wall of the house.   There
had been an attempt to fence in a small front
yard from the vagrant sheep, but slats were few
in the unpainted paling, and the gate hung
loosely by one hinge.   Within was a wild snarl

of cinnamon roses, tansy, butter-and-eggs, and old maid's pinks. A shambling wing ran from the left side of the house. The door was standing open, allowing us to look across the kitchen, through an opposite open door, to the sunny hay-fields beyond. On the window-sill some petunias and geraniums — which should have been long since put in beds — pined in tomato-cans and a couple of broken-nosed teapots. In odd contrast to the shabby yard and shiftless house was a smart silvered glass bell-knob at the kitchen door.

"The front door is beyond argument this time," remarked Mr. Hamlin; and we made our way to the side yard.

Stepping carefully over a rusty pan of meal and water, in which a quarter-grown chicken was wildly floundering, he pulled the bell-knob, which immediately came out in his hand, bringing with it about a yard of wire, and sending the young man violently staggering backward.

After recovering himself, he made another ven-
ture and knocked.   In response to this two
hens appeared from some distant part of the
kitchen and peered at us curiously as if demand-
ing our business; then, finding us of no real
interest, they drifted away, apparently to resume
those domestic employments which our knock
had interrupted.   Just as we were about to try
another knock, a woman was seen crossing the
blazing field beyond the opposite kitchen door.
She entered the kitchen panting and rubicund,
without at first noticing us.

"There now, shoo!" she exclaimed, in a rich
voice and with a lenient manner; "just shoo,
will ye, shoo!   Who give you license to okkipy
the house?   Mebby now, you'd like to be arst
into the fore-room and hev a seat, would n't ye?
Shoo!"

Preceded by a number of scuttling hens, she
came to the door and discovered her visitors.

"Sakes alive!" she said, with a rich chuckling laugh, "I did n't know there was nobody to the door. Comin' in out o' the blaze so, my eyes is sort o' dazzled. Wal, now, I 'm real pleased to see ye. I just ben cross lots to borry some aigs of Mis' Twitchell. Thought I 'd stir up an aig pie for supper. Might think we 'd hev aigs enough of our own to see the hens, but fact is the weasels gets in an' sucks 'em. I told him he 'd oughter mend up the holes, but somehow he haint got round to it. Now do come in an' set down. Here I be runnin' on like old Rideout, an' never puttin' on no manners at all."

"Thank you, we cannot stop," said Mr. Hamlin. "We have brought you some medicine from Dr. Greenleaf."

"Oh, sure enough," said Mrs. Butterfield, "and I 'm sure I 'm real 'bleeged to ye. 'T was for Lowizy's back. The fact is, her cousin Jeduthan Twitchell, he came along ter noon in his old shay, and Lowizy she up an' rid along of him over to the Holler to hear the revivalist speak. I cal'late she 'll feel the need of her medicine afore she gits home. Jeduthan's colt 's got a dreadful pudgicky gait."

" Here," said Mr. Hamlin, contritely, " is your bell-knob. I 'm afraid that I broke it, though I did not mean to pull it too hard."

" Oh, no," she returned reassuringly, " you did n't break it. The children broke it, ringing of it, the same day the lightning-rod man put it in. For my part I was glad, too, when it was finally broke, for such a din as they kep' up with it you never did hear. I told him though that he 'd oughter mend it, but somehow he haint seemed to git round to it."

Mrs. Simeon Butterfield is an ample woman. As she often declared herself: " There was n't no skimpin' when the Lord made me." She is tall, long-limbed, broad-chested, and generously cushioned with flesh, although she is not fat. Not even her limp and loose-hanging calico wrapper could conceal the really fine and Juno-esque lines of her figure. Her hair, which is abundant and of warm, new mahogany color, has the true classic wave; and her throat, which is always collarless, is as white, round, and full as if cut from marble.

"I wish ye would come in now," she still urged. "I can give ye some nice maple-honey that I 've kep ever sence March. Wal, o' course I don't want to urge ye, but you jest wait a minute. You must take a box o' bee-honey along to your par. Sim!"

She had removed her sun-bonnet, and in so doing had brought her hair entirely down. She was now twisting it up, holding her horn "tucking comb" in her teeth for convenience' sake.

"That Sim Butterfield," she said, "is the beatermost for bein' out'n the way when he 's wanted. I s'pose he 's down to the medder lot now, sludgin' round doin' nothin'."

She smiled placidly as she spoke, and did not appear to cherish any animosity toward her husband for his idleness. She disappeared for a few moments, and presently returned and brought to the carriage a gorgeous bunch of peacock's feathers.

"I ben up in the shed chamber," she said pantingly, "after that bee-honey, an' I declare to goodness ef every drop of et haint ben eat up. I feel real mortified. You see the lock to the cupboard was broke a spell ago, an' he haint got round yit to mendin' of it, so I s'pose them young ones hev eat it up. Howsomever, I found these feathers that I 'd put by for ye. You remember our old peacock, 'Jim,' don't ye? You used to set such store by him when you was little an' used to come up with your par. I alwers meant you should have the feathers when Jim was done with 'em, an' old Jim he died last winter. Here! shoo, ye old critter. Don't ye — "

Here Mrs. Butterfield started suddenly across the yard to head a festive young heifer from the corn-field, toward which she was wooed by a tempting gap in the wall; and Jane Savage at the same moment concluded that the visit was at an end, and started quietly down the pasture.

"Our round is ended now," I announced. "Now that dreadful horse may go home again."

"It is a pity," he responded; "I was getting to feel quite like a country doctor. Do you think I would make a good one?"

"No," I answered, with thoughtless quickness. "You are too obstinate, and would insist upon going to the front doors."

"You are always ready to see the worst side of me," he retorted gruffly.

And then he sulked all the way home.

•

VIII.

WHAT BETTY SAYS.

"Lucretia!" I called shrilly, "Lucretia!"

Nobody answered. The tall clock ticked with heavy solemnity. The flies buzzed and droned on the warm, square patch of sunlight that lay on the hall floor, and a little ruby-throated humming-bird made whirring darts at the white bells of Aunt Jane's abutilon, which stood in a green tub on the piazza.

I turned to my companion, who stood leaning against the side of the doorway.

"You see there is nobody at home," I said, "just as I told you. Aunt Jane is gone to carry wheat wafers and elderberry wine to Mrs. Lovel, Lucretia is making calls, and Bobby has gone fishing, so there's nobody at home."

At the sound of my voice, and as if to dispute the truth of what I said, Ned appeared at the parlor door, and after standing a minute with silky ears thrown forward and his lips apart, showing his small white teeth, decided upon the whole to be extravagantly glad to see Mr. Hamlin, and accordingly pranced toward him with a boisterous welcome which consisted chiefly in pretending to eat him up.

"We might go to the orchard," I suggested, when Ned's raptures had subsided. "I was there when you rang the door-bell. It is cool under the trees."

Mr. Hamlin agreeing to this with the air of its not making much difference what he did as long as Lucretia was away, we went to the orchard, with Ned tumbling along ahead of us, now and then stopping to throw us a saucy backward glance, and then starting again with a sudden flounce which made his long ears fly out like wings.

Mr. Hamlin seated himself on the old bench under the seek-no-further tree, and began to sharpen a pencil.

"I'm going to sketch your fine old well-sweep, by your leave," said he.

Mr. Hamlin is very good-looking for so old a man. He has a remarkably straight nose, and honest eyes that look squarely at you when he speaks. His hair is really grayer than Father's, but it is cut so closely that you can hardly see that he has any hair at all. Bob and I like him very well. You seem to get very friendly with a man who is attentive to your sister. After I had finished looking at Mr. Hamlin I turned my attention to the bees, who were rejoicing in the warm afternoon and the fields of clover.

"Why did n't you go fishing with Bob?" asked Mr. Hamlin after a time, without looking up from his sketching.

"Because he was going across the marsh and

would n't take me," I answered, teasing Ned by pulling away the small green apple he was guarding.

"Who did go with him — Fred Harris?"

"Yes," I replied rather crossly, "Fred Harris. Bob seems perfectly happy if he can only get Fred Harris, and Fred *always* scares away the fish."

Mr. Hamlin touched up his sketch and tipped his head a little to look at it.

"You 're not jealous of Fred, I suppose?" he laughed.

"Why, of course not," said I; "it is only that I like to go with Bob, and I can't help feeling that this is our last real boy-and-girl summer together. Bobby goes to college in the fall, you know, and things will never be the same again. Lucretia is going away in the fall, too; she is invited to spend the winter in Boston; and Josephine and Ted will be in New York. I shall be left all alone with dear old Neddy."

"I shall be in Mexico," said Mr. Hamlin.

"Oh, why do you go so far?" I asked bluntly.

"Honor calls, I must obey," he said; "or rather, a good salary calls, and I am a poor man, so I fly to fill a position on the Mexico and El Paso Railway."

"Bob and I are going to Mexico," I announced, "after he graduates. We are going to have a big *hacienda*. Do you know what a *hacienda* is?"

"I think so."

"Well, we're going to have one, and I'm going to keep house for Bob, and he's going to lasso wild horses, and I shall write a book about the people."

"Perhaps you might take me to board," suggested Mr. Hamlin.

"Perhaps we will — if you are not married."

"Rooms to let to single gentlemen only?" laughed he. "Well, all right. I shall not be married."

He said it quite positively; and it occurred to me that this was a good chance to free my mind of something that I wished to say regarding Lucretia. I could see plainly that Mr. Hamlin was already rather fond of Lucretia, though of course he's old enough to be her father. I might have been willing if he'd been settled in New York, but I just wanted him to understand that Lucretia was far too dainty and pretty to marry a man who would take her to Mexico.

"I am glad you are not going to marry," I said abruptly.

"Why?" asked he, looking amused.

"Because," I answered, "it is so dreadfully selfish for a man to ask a nice, pretty, accomplished girl to leave her pleasant, civilized home, and go off into the wilderness with him, where she can't have anybody to speak to, and Apaches scalp her, and howl about nights, and everything is as horrid as it can be."

"It really is n't a very charming picture," he

said. "It is just as well, then, that I do not think of marrying, is n't it?"

He must have spoiled his sketch, for he twitched out the leaf he was drawing on, and crumpled it up and gave it to Ned.

"Oh," I cried, "I wanted to see it."

"It was no good," he said.

Ned's disposition is such that he cannot usually enjoy anything if he thinks he has a right to do so. Mr. Hamlin pretended to try to recover the paper; and the spaniel worried and twitched at it and finally raced with it around the corner of the house, whence he came instantly tumbling back with Bevis Sparhawk.

Behind Bevis came his mother, under a huge parasol of black lace and satin.

"I 've been ringing at your nasty bell for ages," she called out cheerfully. "Where is your remarkable maid?"

She sat down in Father's steamer chair, closed her sunshade, put up her eyeglasses, and began

to wave a beautiful fan of black ostrich plumes.
She was dressed entirely in black, — thin, delicate black, unrelieved by any touch of color.
She looked very elegant, and made me all at
once conscious of being very young and having
a frowzly head and a tumbled gown.

"For my part," declared Mr. Hamlin, "I
don't believe they really have any maid. I
might be ringing there still if Miss Betty had
not heard me from some far-off hammock and
come to my rescue."

"Oh, yes," said Mrs. Sparhawk, seriously,
" they really have a maid, I assure you, and a
charmingly unique one, too; so delightfully
grim, a perfect martinet, and the way in which
she bullies the family is perfectly delicious."

"She came sixteen years ago when mother
died," I ventured. " Bobby and I were only
babies then, and she has done everything for
us, so she is almost like one of the family."

"Which means, you know," added Mrs. Sparhawk, "that she dares to give her opinion upon all occasions, and say quite as nasty things as one's relatives would. She is not a servant at all, you know, but a person of importance with money in the Canal Bank and stock in the Grand Trunk Railway. She always attires herself in all her Sunday awfulness of array, and takes a free ride to Portland on stockholders' day!"

It is one of the curious things about Mrs. Sparhawk that she always unconsciously takes things into her own hands. I had thought that I was doing very well at entertaining Mr. Hamlin, but now I suddenly found Mrs. Sparhawk acting the part of the gracious hostess, while I sat meekly by and allowed her to describe Harriet, who had lived with us for years, and whom she probably never saw more than half a dozen times. I felt like a guest in our own orchard, and a very unimportant guest at that.

"I'm doin' wis you, too," announced Bevis,

who had been for some time trying to get a chance to speak.

"Now, Bevis Sparhawk," said his mother, "did n't I tell you that you were *not* to talk? That is why I abominate making visits with children," she added, turning to Mr. Hamlin; "they always want to talk, and one wants to do the talking one's self, don't you know, and so of course — "

"I 'm a doin' wis you, too," repeated Bevis, shrilly, trying to drown his mother's voice; "me and Wodney, and little black Sam, and mammy an' — an' — "

"No, you will not, you tiresome child," said Mrs. Sparhawk, "unless you behave yourself and stop interrupting."

"You did it you'sef," said the warlike Bevis; "you 'poke an' 'poke when I was a-'peakin'."

"The truth is," said she, turning to us, and ignoring her son's remark, "that is the very reason that I called to-day. I wanted to ask your father and your sister what they would say to our taking the children."

"Where? To Sippican!" I asked.

"Yes," she replied cheerfully, "to Sippican. Now, pray do not credit me with making such a diabolical plan; it was all the Colonel, I assure you. He positively adores those children, don't you know. He absolutely cannot be happy without them. Now, I am different. Of course, I worship the children, simply idolize them, you know; but then I'm philosophical, and I can endure life for a week or two without them; but the Colonel is set upon their going."

"I think it would be very jolly indeed," said Mr. Hamlin. "I dare say the change would be for their health."

"Heavens!" exclaimed Mrs. Sparhawk, devoutly, "I hope not, I'm sure. They are frightfully healthy already, and they eat like a swarm of grasshoppers. Seriously, I've had thoughts of dosing them with sulphur, or making them learn hymns, or something nasty, just to tone down their spirits. — Bevis Sparhawk, you cruel child, stop pulling that poor dog's ears, or I 'll feed you on gunpowder."

"Then," returned the unmoved Bevis, struggling with Ned for a bit of bone, "I shall be a gun, and dead you. I want sumpin' to eat."

"How is your uncle's health now, Mr. Hamlin?" asked Mrs. Sparhawk, suddenly abandoning Bevis. "He was such a delightful old gentleman. They make one feel so young and blooming, don't you know? Your uncle was quite one of the old school."

It seemed to me somehow that Mr. Hamlin was not particularly interested in his uncle, and it also seemed that Mrs. Sparhawk was so much interested in him that I rather doubted her having called about the children. Perhaps I was suspicious, but I could not help fancying that she had seen Mr. Hamlin over the hedge and had come in on purpose to talk to him.

" I want sumpin' to eat," said Bevis once more.

" No, you do not, you ill-bred child," said his mother. " Does your uncle still keep bachelor's hall in that exquisite house of his in Baltimore? "

" I will have sumpin' to eat," insisted Bevis.

" Bevis Sparhawk, you will not have one crumb to eat. — No, Miss Betty, thank you, not a crumb. — If you say one more word about it I shall take you home and shut you up in the rabbit hutch. — I was at the Carrollton," continued Mrs. Sparhawk, blandly, " and mamma was with me. She was alarmingly ill, and — Oh, Miss Betty, if you would give that detestable child a cake, I should adore you forever."

Upon this Bevis and I departed for the house. We found that Aunt Jane had returned from her visit, and she was so delighted at a chance to bestow dainties that she overwhelmed the joyous

Bevis with seed-cakes and her choicest sugared cherries.

Lucretia came in, too, drawing off her pretty pearl-gray gloves.

" I made nine calls," she said complacently.

" You must have had *very* good luck in finding them out," said I, enviously.

" I really think," fluttered Aunt Jane, " that we ought to offer some refreshments. Lucretia, go out to your company. Betty can stay and help me."

After Mrs. Sparhawk and Mr. Hamlin had partaken of pound cakes and Russian tea and departed, Ned came rushing by me, trying to make me take away from him a crumpled bit of paper. It was all that was left of Mr. Hamlin's sketch. If it was the well-sweep, it had a hat on. If he was making a picture of Lucretia, why could n't he have been honest about it, and said so? I 'm sure I should have liked to see it myself.

IX.

WHAT BOB SAYS.

I WAS over in the little north lot yesterday, trying to find some squirrels or something else to shoot. I was all alone.

It was about noon and blazing hot, and along the walls, somewhere behind the blackberry bushes, a quail was whistling "more wet." Every time the quail whistled Ned would make a crazy dash, barking loud enough to scare away every bird in America. Betty has just ruined Ned for a bird dog, anyway. Women always spoil a dog. I had n't shot a thing the whole morning, and was lying down under a jolly big birch-tree to cool off and rest a bit before starting for home, when all of a sudden Ned jumped up, ran a few steps, stopped, threw his ears forward, and said "Woof!" The next second I heard an awful howl, and running to the open field found Rodney Sparhawk dancing about like a young lunatic, and shrieking that Bevis was drowned and "all deaded."

"Where is he?" asked I, rushing for him.

"In the river all deaded up," said Rodney.

It is n't a river, it is only a shallow brook; but sure enough, Bevis Sparhawk was in it, sitting on the stony bottom and howling away like a young Pawnee. He was so sure he was going to drown that he had n't tried to help himself at all. I picked him out, and he said he was sitting on a stone catching "minnies" in the skirt of his dress, and Rodney had pushed him in. Rodney said he did n't do it; that he was only trying to get on the stone with Bevis. Anyhow, the two little beggars were wet as polliwogs, and had evidently run away; so I raced them back home with me, and they were nearly dry by the time we reached the village.

When we came to the house we found doors

and windows wide open as usual, and Mrs. Sparhawk was in the parlor, fainting away on a sofa, or pretending to, and saying that her darlings were dead, and she should never see them again. The Colonel and the old darky woman were fanning her and trying to brace her up.

"I know my darlings have been stolen," said she; "I shall never see them any more. Oh, my darlings, my babies!"

"Bevis was drownded, but he's a great deal better now," said Rodney, bursting in.

"I taught a fiss for you, but his tail was so slippy he swimmed away," said Bevis, shrilly.

Upon this they all made a rush for the children, and Mrs. Sparhawk sat up on her sofa. Of course I was backing out myself, but I heard what she said.

"You miserable little green baboons!" cried she, "how dared you run away and give me such a fright? I shall be ill from the shock,

I 've no doubt. You deserve a thorough whipping, both of you, you nasty, untidy little pirates. I 'm sure, Colonel, I hope you are proud of your children *now!*"

Just then unluckily she caught sight of me, and so she said no end of silly things.

"You must stay and tell me all about it, and have some coffee," said she; and it was no use for a fellow to say there was nothing to tell, because she seemed to have made her mind up to make me stay. She sent the black woman off for coffee, and the children off to bed; but I think they only had dry clothes on; at any rate, they were eating cookies on the front steps when I went out a little later.

Mrs. Sparhawk sat down and began to fan herself.

"It is exactly like those nasty little apes to go and drown themselves on a day when I am expecting company," said she. "Limkin, I think you may give me a *soupçon* of cognac in my coffee, my nerves are so shattered."

One good thing about Mrs. Sparhawk is that she treats a fellow with some respect. She does n't call me "Bobby" and act as if I 'd no right to be about anyhow.

After the coffee came, the Colonel excused himself and took his cup up in his studio; and Mrs. Sparhawk poured my cup twice as strong as Aunt Jane ever gives it to me. There were little crackers, too, and a crimson cheese that Mrs. Sparhawk dug pieces out of with a little silver spade. She did put a spoonful of brandy in her coffee, though she made fun of herself for doing it, and said one learned bad tricks in the army.

She was talking about fishing, and she asked me if she did not see me one morning coming back with Mr. Hamlin. So I told her "yes," and how many we caught; and she seemed to take a good deal of interest in Hamlin, and asked me no end of questions about him; but of course I don't know much about him; so then she began to tell me about her company, — a city girl that she has sent for. She said she wanted us all to be very polite to her, but I think myself it is too great a pity she's coming, because we were just a nice party before. But of course I didn't tell Mrs. Sparhawk so, and after a while she let me go.

I can't write any more now because Fred is standing outside throwing his baseball up at the window, and he'll plug it through a pane of glass in a minute if I don't go and stop him.

X.

WHAT BETTY SAYS.

My pretty Lucretia came tripping down the stairs, and stopped a minute at the parlor door.

"Why, Betty Greenleaf!" said she, "are n't you ready for Sabbath-school?"

"She cannot go," said Aunt Jane, with plaintive severity; "she must needs go to meddling with Robert's tools — and on a Sunday too — and she has cut her hand with the screw-driver."

"She was fixing a nail in her shoe," spoke Bob, in friendly defence; "but then she was a gump to let the screw-driver slip, — just like a girl."

"At any rate I cannot go to Sunday-school, Lucretia," said I, being at length allowed to speak a word for myself. "You can see that I cannot get a glove on."

Lucretia's smooth white forehead drew itself into a frown.

"I do hate to go alone, Betty," she said forlornly; "I never like to go alone to Sunday-school."

She looked very pretty in her crisp summer bravery. She was dainty and exquisite from bonnet to boot, and I could n't help hoping that Mr. Hamlin might somehow chance to see her.

"You will be late, Lucretia, if you do not go at once," said Aunt Jane; "Sister Buzzell went by some time ago, and you know she is usually tardy."

"Yes, I suppose I must go," said Lucretia, dubiously.

She gathered up her pretty lilac muslin, unfurled her sun-umbrella, and reluctantly stepped forth into the blazing afternoon. It was two

o'clock.   The house was so quiet that one could
hear the solemn tick of the entry timepiece and
the rustle of the pages of Bob's book.   Father
was asleep on the old lounge in the front entry,
with a red bandanna laid over his face.   Harriet
Tuell had gone to a baptism at Stony Brook.
Bob was reading " Scottish Chiefs " for the
fortieth time.   He was lying face downward
upon the wide old couch; his chin rested in
his hands, and his right foot dangled uncomfortably to the floor.   Aunt Jane sat by a south
window.   She wore her best black gown because it was Sunday, and she had a bunch of
her favorite mignonette in a glass on the sill
beside her.   She was reading a little book
called " Why Am I a Universalist; " and she
looked, as she always does, very much like a
little white mouse that Bobby and I once had.
Everybody seemed to be content and occupied
except myself.   I was not sleepy, and I had
nothing to read.

"I say, Betty," said Bob, "let up rapping on the window, will you?"

I stopped obediently. A humming-bird came to call upon the white abutilon, and uttered fine, fairy-like cries of rapture as it darted at the golden-hearted bells. Ned appeared round the corner quietly, and having deposited upon the front steps a particularly disreputable shoe, gazed at it a moment admiringly and departed with a satisfied air of duty done. The sight of the dog and the cheering sound of a little breeze inspired me.

"Let's go to the old grave-yard, Bob," I whispered, glancing toward Aunt Jane, who had placidly gone to sleep without discovering why she was a Universalist.

"Not now," replied Bob, rather crossly, "I'm reading. Get something to do, Betty, can't you, and let a fellow alone."

Being snubbed by my chief ally, I tiptoed after my hat, called Ned, and started forth on

9

the only correct and orthodox Sunday walk for
Arrowsic folk, — that to the old grave-yard.

Down the village street we went together,
Ned walking sedately for the space of a moment, then rushing ahead with wildly flying
ears, and stopping short to wait for me with
a look of irresistible waggishness. We went
through a gate, unpainted and rusty-hinged,
into a lane bordered by stone walls and rough
with grass-grown ruts; then through an ancient
stile and into the sunny, peaceful precincts of
the old cemetery. Usually this is quite a
lively place of a Sunday afternoon, with rustic
lovers and pairs of chattering girls; but yesterday the superior attractions of the immersion
at Stony Brook had left the old grave-yard
empty, and Ned and I had it quite to ourselves
for a time. Ned settled down to a season of
solid enjoyment in chasing white and yellow
butterflies. I sat upon the dry, warm grass,
smoothed out my gown, folded my hands, and

enjoyed the sights and sounds of the lovely summer afternoon.

After a time Ned grew tired and went to sleep, with his muzzle resting on his silky brown paws. I was almost asleep myself, I think, the bees sounded so far away, when somebody spoke behind me and made me jump.

"Can you inform me how long an Arrowsic Sunday usually is?" said a voice, and Mr. Hamlin in a very nice gray suit came down and faced me.

He held his cane in both hands horizontally behind him, and looked good-natured but rather tired.

"They are *years* long," I answered, "unless Bob happens to be good-natured; then they are shorter."

"And if you happened not to have any Bob?" he asked.

"Then I should *die*," I replied seriously.

" People do not, unfortunately, find it so easy to die," said he. " May I sit down? "

" Of course you can if you want to," I said, not very politely, but he did not seem to mind.

He put down his cane and took off his round straw hat. I always look at his hair with surprise, it is so gray. I did not realize that I was staring very rudely until he looked up and asked if his hair was in disorder.

" It could n't be," I said, laughing, " it is too short. I was wondering how it could be so gray when — "

" When I am so young and fair? " he finished seriously. " My mother was white-haired at seventeen."

" Mrs. Sparhawk," I volunteered, " had her hair bleached in Paris. When she first came here to live it was quite blond, like Lucretia's."

" It must have been atrociously unbecoming."

" On the contrary, she looked well with it, and she explained to every lady quite openly how it was done. I like Mrs. Sparhawk, she is so very amusing. We Arrowsic people are not at all amusing. We are well-behaved and dull."

" Cannot one be well-behaved, then, and amusing, too?" asked Mr. Hamlin, taking out his sketching book, which seemed to be his constant companion.

"I don't know," I said doubtfully; "there is Aunt Jane, and Harriet,—though to be sure Harriet is amusing, but she does n't mean to be. Mrs. Sparhawk means to be, and she told Lucretia that she was interested in you on account of your uncle."

Mr. Hamlin put on his glasses, which at once transformed him from a pleasant and cheerful young man to a supercilious and cynical person ten years beyond his usual age.

"She makes a sad mistake," he said rather gently, " if she adopts me on his account. She would please him much better by sending me to Coventry at once without delay."

For some minutes he sat silent, drawing an
outline of the long range of the White Hills,
which loomed large and hazy against the summer sky. Presently his face changed, and he
looked up with a cheerful smile.

"I don't know why I should care," he said,
"but somehow I do whenever I remember it.
Come, Miss Betty, shall I tell you the strange
history of the ' Boy who would not study
Greek '? "

"If you will," I answered; "I am fond of
stories."

"This is rather a stupid one; however, I
believe I will bore you with it. As Hans Ander-
sen says, ' Now listen.' There was once a good
little boy — "

"Good?" I queried.

"*Very* good. Do not be sceptical, Miss
Betty, and do not interrupt. It is rude in the
extreme. There was once, then, a *very* good
little boy, who lived in a house in the city of

Baltimore, all alone with his widowed mother and his uncle. The mother was a placid, gentle little soul, who was fond of old lace, lived upon macaroons, and painted butterflies on rice paper for occupation. The uncle was a queer old stick, — rich, but irascible. Do you know what ' irascible ' means?"

"Of course," I replied indignantly.

"Very well. The uncle, then, was rich, but irascible, and was in the habit of blustering about like the regulation old stage tyrant, and boasting that he would be master in his own house; that his 'will was law,' or words to that effect. Well, the boy went to school, of course, and was fitting for the classical course in the college where his father had gone, and his uncle, and all his grandfathers for generations back. He had got as far in Latin as ' *Arma virumque cano*,' and was grubbing away sullenly at Greek roots, when all of a sudden, one day, it popped into his head that there was really no sort of reason in his wasting his time over anything that he detested so cordially."

" He was a conceited little boy," I said decidedly, " to think that he could judge of what he ought to study. I 'm glad you 're not telling this mutinous story to Bob."

" I will tell it to Bob if you interrupt me, Miss Betty. Well, so the boy simply did not learn any Greek lesson that day, and when he was called up to recite, announced that he had stopped studying Greek. The master, with some interest, inquired when he had stopped, and the boy replied, ' About half an hour ago.' "

" What a horrid, impertinent boy ! "

" Now I shall tell Bob. However, the master agreed with you, and, finding that his own remarks did not make much impression, proceeded to go and break the news to the uncle. Then the uncle ranted about in gorgeous style, as you may imagine ; for you see the trouble was that, although the uncle was the boy's legal guardian, there was a certain clause in the will which directed that after he was fifteen years old he should be allowed to choose his own profession. 'You'll never make a lawyer unless you study Greek, sir!' said the uncle. The boy replied that he did n't intend to be a lawyer, but a civil engineer. At this time there was a worse row than ever. Even the little mother joined the charge, and cried, and asked the boy if he 'wanted to disgrace the family and break his mother's heart, and grow up and be hung. There had been a lawyer in every generation, and now he was going to break the line and ruin his father's good name.' But the boy was a stubborn cub, and the upshot of the whole thing was that the uncle flew into a white rage. He was obliged to send the boy to an Institute of Technology, but he never spoke to him again, not even when the mother died; and for six years the two men have never met."

"How dreadful!" I said, as Mr. Hamlin,

having finished his tale, began to sharpen his lead pencil.

" Not so **very** dreadful," he replied coolly. " He is, to be sure, my only living relative, but he is happy in his way, and I in mine. He has, or thinks he has, the best collection of old lacquer in the world; and I have my profession and some good friends; so what does it matter?"

" But he is your father's brother," I urged. " I should go to see him sometime."

" And be accused, as I was once by letter, of having an eye to his money. No, I thank you."

" I say," said a voice behind us, " Father is called to the Hollow, and we 're having an early tea; and you 'd better come home, Betty Greenleaf, if you know when you 're well off."

" Don't scold," laughed Mr. Hamlin, putting away his sketch-book; " we refuse to feel guilty. Why, the sun is an hour above Mount Kearsage yet."

XI.

HERE we are, safe at Camp Sippican at last, though I really began to think that we never should get here. First, Bevis Sparhawk had the mumps; then Josephine's mother had to go to Sweden to see her married daughter; and then, just as we were all ready to start, it began to rain cats and dogs, and never let up a minute for a whole week. But at last it managed to clear off, and yesterday morning we really got started.

There was Joel Jackson and the express wagon, with the tents and Fred and me; we started first of all, for the rest kept forgetting things and going back, and waiting for each other, and behaving like a set of crazy coots generally. The Fosters' beach wagon took Hamlin

and Lucretia and Ted, and Amos to drive the
horses back.   Then the Dudleys came in their
chaise, and Emily squeezed in the middle of the
seat; and the Winthrop carryall had Mr. and
Mrs. Winthrop and Arthur and the young lady
that is visiting the Sparhawks, because the Sparhawk carriage was running over with Rodney
and Bevis.   Betty came up with Father in his
old chaise.   I thought they sort of left her out
in the cold; but I suppose there was n't any
room for her in the Fosters' wagon, and Betty
seemed to be as cheerful as ever, so I don't
know that it made any difference.

We got there first of all.   Fred says that he 's
always taken notice that horses go slower when
there are girls in the carriage, and I guess it is
true.   At any rate, we got to Sippican a good
hour before any other carriage showed up
at all.

When you get to Sippican you see a hum-
mocky pasture at your left, and just beyond the

pasture the mountain begins. Then on the right of the road is the camping ground, — a jolly big field with two or three apple-trees in one end, — wild fruit, you know, no good to eat, — and from the road this field runs down to Sippican Pond. Sippican is an old Indian name, you know, and means " Clear Water," and so the mountain was named after the pond. You could n't find a completer camping ground in the whole country. For there is the pond, you see, where you can catch jolly pickerel, and then the other side of the mountain is a trout brook, and there is an ice-cold spring in the woods near by, and plenty of wood to burn, so you could n't find a better place, anyhow.

Fred and I helped Joel put up the tents, and of course the rest of the fellows worked when they got along. We have good board floors all ready to fit right together, and the tents are none of your cheap affairs, but regular out-and-out good ones. There are three big ones,

and a smaller one that we call the galley, only
we don't cook in it unless it is a pouring
rain, because fish smell nicer cooked out of
doors.

A good deal depends on how you start, in
camping out; and we know just how to fix our
tents. We make the floors good and even, and
we put up the tents as strong as they can be
fixed. Of course, though, we always go about
at night and see to them and pound down the
pins. They bring rugs for the floors, and ticks
all ready to be filled up at the Burnham farm-
house with nice clean straw. We keep the
horses up there, too; the ones that are n't sent
home, I mean. Of course we did n't get everything done last night, but we got all the tents
built. We have a kerosene stove, but I think
the regular camp-fire is jollier, and we always
have that lighted in the evening, anyway, for
company. Of course last night we had our
supper off the things we brought from home.

Mrs. Winthrop is head cook, and Mr. Winthrop and Fred and I helped.

Mrs. Dudley and Emily and Betty set the table. We had cold ham and bread and pickles and doughnuts and cheese and apple-puffs and hot baked potatoes and coffee, and a heap more things; and you can believe that first supper just tasted good, though, with the fire blazing away, and the loon crying over the water, and the cool wind coming along the field, and Aunt Jane not there to say that a fellow stuck his elbows out when he cut his ham.

XII.

WHAT BETTY SAYS.

WITH two pillows, a bag, a blanket, a pair of rubbers, and a lantern, I crept uncomfortably under the closed fly of a tent, inside of which things certainly presented an appearance which Harriet would have scornfully denounced as " mixed an' mingled." I had been sent for various necessary and unnecessary articles to the still unpacked trunks, which stood in the dining-tent, and had now before me the task of making my bed for the first night's rest at Sippican. Lucretia, in a most becoming blue dressing-gown, her flossy yellow hair all about her shoulders, was sitting on the edge of her straw bed putting up crimps in company with Josephine Foster. Emily Dudley, who is the most matter-of-fact and common-place of mortals, was already soundly asleep. Mrs. Dudley, whose hobby is to be always taking doses herself and offering them to others, had put on a plaid flannel dressing-gown, and above this a jacket of quilted cashmere.

"Thank you very much for finding my rubbers," she said, as I came in. "I do not dare to go to sleep without them. They will draw the soles of my feet, perhaps, but I dare not risk the damp air striking my feet. The boards of the floor are by no means properly seasoned."

"Now I'll tell you a story," announced a cheerful voice from a distant corner: "Once they was free child'n, all black, and would n't eat their suppers; so the great big bear came a roarin' and a growlin', and *wow!* he eated them all up but they bones, and he eated them up too!"

"Rodney Sparhawk, you tiresome child," exclaimed Mrs. Sparhawk, "don't let me hear another word from you to-night. Do you understand?"

"Then I'll whisker, so you can't hear me," said the unquenched Rodney.

"Don't want to be eated all up with a bear," piped Bevis, dismally.

"There are no bears at all," said his mother, "and Rodney is nasty to tell stories to frighten you. Go to sleep, and hurry about it, or all the sweet little dreams will fly away from your bed."

"Do you see any now?" queried Bevis, with anxiety.

"Yes, a great many lovely ones."

"But I can't see them."

"That is because you do not wear glasses. Now go to sleep this minute."

"All wight," replied Bevis, drowsily.

By this time Mrs. Dudley had put up her curl papers and solemnly tied on a quilted hood. Next she bound bits of scarlet flannel about her wrists to guard against rheumatism, took two pills and a dose of some nauseous-looking yellow mixture from a bottle, put out her little safety-lamp, and finally retired. Silence settled over the tent, and over the encampment. Everybody was either asleep or trying to get to sleep; but as for me, I was never more hopelessly wide-awake. I tossed about on my straw bed and changed my pillow from side to side. The night air stole in under the tent, cool and damp and sweet. Josephine Foster sneezed unwarily. Instantly a match was scratched, the safety-lamp glimmered in the darkness like a little star, and Mrs. Dudley came across the tent.

" Open your mouth," she said, in a voice which sounded deep and hollow in the silence.

No reply from Josephine, though I think she was not asleep. Mrs. Dudley grasped her shoulder firmly.

"Wake up," she said; "open your mouth and take this."

"Take what?" asked Josephine, sleepily.

"A quinine pill. You sneezed, and I think there's probably malaria around. Or are you having a chill?"

"I am not," said Josephine, ungratefully. "I am not the least bit chilly. I am too warm under this great blanket."

"Then you must be feverish," said Mrs. Dudley, triumphantly, "and that is a much worse symptom."

"I have n't any symptoms at all, Mrs. Dudley," said Josephine, with sleepy rudeness, "and I shall not take any medicine at all."

Upon this Mrs. Dudley retired to her couch in injured silence, and sleep once more settled upon all eyelids but my own. Some perverse imp seemed to have taken upon himself the special charge of keeping my eyes open and my ears unnaturally alert. Once the floor creaked strangely. Then there was little to hear except the many chirping voices of the insects of a summer night, merged into a sort of out-door orchestra. I lay separating the sounds. That was the tree-toad; that the cricket; that the katydid; those the whistles of the frogs in the marshes; that "glug! chunck!" was some portly dweller among the sword reeds and blue flag on the pond's border. In any pause came the soft, hissing lap of the water, running up over the tiny beach and then sliding musically back again. Perhaps it was this sound which first made me imagine I was thirsty. It was only imagination, to begin with, but once indulging, I found myself becoming more miserable every minute. I thought of the terrible pictures by Doré in Father's "Ancient Mariner." I saw distinctly the ghastly faces, the open mouths, the hideous protruding tongues and eyeballs. I was growing quite wild with nervousness and thirst, when something happened which made me forget myself and my discomfort completely. Just outside the tent I heard a soft and stealthy footstep. It was very deliberate, but it came nearer and nearer every minute. It was most uncomfortable to lie there listening to the sound, and to feel that I was the only waking, hearing being in the whole dark camp. In a moment *something* touched the tent canvas and moved along cautiously as if feeling for the door. Just then a hand from Emily Dudley's bed grasped me.

"Do you hear that?" whispered Emily, hoarsely.

"Yes," I answered. "What do you think it is? There used to be bears on Sippican. You don't think — "

"Of course not, silly," said the practical Emily. "It is a tramp or something, and he will rob the provision tent. I must manage to go and call Father."

Just here came a stumble. Our tent quaked wildly, and some heavy body fell to the ground with violence.

"Oh, come now!" exclaimed a masculine voice, which ran unexpectedly into a squeak at the end.

The feeling of utter relief was delightful. I slipped on my rubber sandals, and wrapped in my big gray blanket, hastened silently from the tent.

"Oh, Bobby," I said, "is it you?"

"Of course," replied Bob, crossly, "who did you think?"

"What are you doing?"

"Trying to be still, and not wake anybody up."

"Did you tumble over a guy rope?" I giggled delightedly.

"Of course I did," returned Bob, with some sharpness, "but it does n't strike me as so awfully funny as it seems to you. I am on my way to the dining tent after a dipper."

"Oh, if you are going for water," I said joyously, all my thirst returning, "I will go too.

I can find a glass or a dipper, or something, because I put them away."

We made our way to the dining tent. As I crept in under the door I caught a curious glow or flash on the floor, which at once disappeared. I stood still, with my heart pounding against my side. There was a tramp about then, as Emily had thought, and he was here in the tent, alone in the darkness with me. I fortified myself by thinking of Bob, who was waiting close outside.

"Who is here?" I demanded, in a feeble and shaky voice.

After an instant of silence there was a little click. The faint glow appeared again, and I saw Miss Alexander, Mrs. Sparhawk's guest, sitting upon the floor, with a tiny dark lantern beside her. She looked unnaturally white, and her large, pale-blue eyes shone like a cat's. She had a dark cloak about her, and her wavy red hair was tumbling over her shoulders.

"Are you ill?" I asked. "I thought you were in our tent asleep."

"I could not sleep," she said softly and hurriedly. "I crept out and came here. I must write a letter for Jackson to carry back to-morrow. But no one must know. I am sure I can trust you, Miss Betty; you will not betray me?"

"I will not tell," I said stiffly, for I thought she was silly, and that she was trying to make a mystery out of a very simple matter. Of course Mrs. Sparhawk would not have minded her writing a letter.

"Oh, thank you," she said very earnestly; "I thought I could trust you. I was sure I could."

I made no answer, and by the time I had found a mug she was busily writing by the pale glow of her little lantern.

"What were you talking to yourself about, Betty?" asked Bob, as I joined him.

"I could n't find the glasses," I answered, evasively, "and I was hunting about for them. Ugh! how cold the grass is!"

It was cold and quite drenched with dew, and I shivered a little as we stood on the tiny white beach. The water of the pond looked black as ink, and now and then we caught a faint splash out on its sullen surface, from some leaping fish or elfish water-sprite. Bob dipped a cupful of the cool liquid, and impolitely drank first, before dipping any for me.

"It tastes mighty froggy," he said critically.

I crept quietly back into the tent. I wondered if Miss Alexander had come in before me; but I did not speculate much, for soon the crickets ceased their chirping, my thoughts became deliciously confused, and I slipped away into a dreamless sleep.

XIII.

WHAT BOB SAYS.

I SAY that it comes hard on a fellow to be everlastingly sitting down to write, when there are so many better things to do. If you were a girl it would n't matter, and Betty need not take on airs just because her chapters are longer than mine. She is n't a man, and it does n't depend on her whether we have any meat for dinner.

The ham and beef are all gone, you see, and the tongue, too. So now we have got to shoot our own dinners. It is against the law to buy any meat. Fred and I went away up the brook to-day and caught a jolly lot of trout. They are sizzling away now, over the fire, and Betty is peeling the potatoes. Mr. Dudley always makes the coffee, and I can tell you it smells

good enough.   We shall have blueberries, too,
for supper, that we picked on the mountain to-
day.   After supper those that dare to, go row-
ing in the punt; she leaks, but Fred and I are
going to patch her up.   We can fix her, I think,
so that, at least, the water won't come in faster
than you can bail it out.   There are water-lilies
over across the pond; only the beaver lilies,
the yellow kind, grow on this side.

Supper is ready at last, so I can't write any
more.

XIV.

WHAT BETTY SAYS.

IN the high heat of a summer afternoon we were toiling dismally up the rough side of Sippican Mountain. The path wound among rocky ledges and clumps of hemlock and blueberry. There was no shade until one reached the evergreen belt, half-way to the summit. It was a day of sickening heat, without a puff of wind, and our party was rather silent as we languidly trailed along in single file, "going to fish for blueberries," as Bob wittily remarked.

"I am not going one single step farther," announced Lucretia, suddenly.

She sat down hopelessly on a cushion of crisp gray moss, and took off her hat. Her face was as pink as a wild rose; and her hair, usually knotted so closely, was loosened just enough to free a few pretty, soft locks about her neck and face. Lucretia was only flushed enough to look adorably pretty. I was conscious myself of being most vulgarly crimson-faced and blowzy.

"If you give up, Lucretia, then so shall I," said Josephine, fretfully. "I wish I had stayed at camp. I'm sure I never should have dreamed of coming, if I had known how warm it was."

She also sat down and removed her hat. Ted and Colonel Sparhawk urged them to try to reach the pines, and a sympathetic group gathered about them. Just before me Emily Dudley plodded with an air of stolid endurance, and ahead of her Mr. Hamlin was wandering on by himself, looking very ill-natured.

"The only truly sensible members of the camp are those who refused to come on this direful scramble," said a voice behind, and Arthur Winthrop joined me.

His round face was crimson with heat, and his spectacles reflected the sunshine dazzlingly.

"I am looking for geodes," he announced cheerfully, — "garnet geodes. I have heard they are found on Sippican, though I am bound to say I never found one myself."

Arthur Winthrop is just out of college. He is a painfully good and studious young man. He always does what is expected of him, and it is his mother's placid boast that "Arty" has never caused her an hour's anxiety since he was born.

"I have not devoted my whole time to geology," he said, "for I have been cutting alpenstocks for the young ladies. Here is one for you. It will help you up the hill."

"Did you cut your initials on them all?" I asked, as I accepted the gift.

"No," he replied, with kind patronage; "that was a special favor to you."

We had reached the pine belt by this time,

and were sitting down to rest in the shade. Below us the rest of the party had abandoned the intention of sitting forever on the blazing hillside. They were toiling toward us silently in single file, except that Theodore was helping Lucretia.

" Come," said the relentless voice of Emily Dudley above me, " if you stop at all, you 'll begin to realize how warm and tired you are. Just keep right on, and you won't mind it half so much."

Arthur Winthrop remonstrated, but I rose obediently.

"We shall have no hot cakes for supper if we do not get the berries," I said sordidly.

"I do not think of cakes at a time like this," reproved my companion.

Nevertheless, I left him sitting on a bank of moss, and keeping away the mosquitoes with a brake, while I followed Emily and presently emerged from the pines into the sunlight once more. Here were the berries, however, — covering the bushes, growing in fat clusters, each berry as large as a small grape, and covered with lovely blue bloom. Mr. Hamlin had taken his field-glass and disappeared. Emily and I were apparently all alone on the top of Sippican Mountain. Emily Dudley picked berries with the steady, persistent method with which she does everything. She entirely cleared one bush of fruit before leaving it, and never wandered about for "thick places," as Bob and I do.

After a while I found myself out of sight of Emily. It grew hotter and stiller on the mountain. I could no longer hear the voices of Ted and Arthur singing "Lauriger" below in the woods. Only the harsh cawing of a pair of crows, sweeping about over their great nest in a blasted pine-tree, broke the stillness. They, too, became quiet, and I heard my own heavy breathing and the rattle of the berries falling into my tin pail.

Presently I remembered that Bob and Fred
were fishing at a pond somewhere beyond this
side of the mountain, and I became quite eager
to see the water. I wandered here and there
for different views. I did not find the pond,
which was not wholly strange, as I was constantly going lower instead of higher. I sat
down to rest presently, discouraged by the
distance I had come. One comes so much
more swiftly down a mountain than one can
climb up. I began to eat up my blueberries,
which were warm but luscious. High above
me, at my left, a grateful little cloud shadowed
the sun for a moment. From the same direction came a shrill Swiss yodel, repeated several
times, and in a moment Mr. Hamlin appeared
and came down, stumbling and sliding over
stones and the smooth, dry grass.

"I have brought you an alpenstock," he
cried.

"I have one already," I said ungraciously,

as he came beside me. " I mean, of course, I am much obliged, but you see Arthur Winthrop gave me one."

Mr. Hamlin sat down on the crisp gray moss beside me, and taking up my alpenstock, regarded it a little scornfully.

" It is crooked," he said.

It was as straight as a dart, but I did not defend it.

" Did you ask him to cut his initials on it? " he asked.

" No," I replied meekly.

" Then what business had he to do it? "

" They are very good letters," I said critically.

" He might as well have made them all slant the same way, while he was about it," observed Mr. Hamlin.

" They do," I said half-heartedly, for I was becoming dissatisfied with my stick.

" He might at least have smoothed the top off a little better," went on my companion;

"however, if you have one, you don't want another;" and he was about to fling his staff away.

"Oh, don't!" I cried, "please do not. I think I would rather have it. It — I think yours is straighter."

"Well, give me the other, then. You cannot keep both. One must go."

Reluctantly, and fully aware of my own baseness, I gave up poor Arthur's stick, with all its careful carving, and saw it sent, with a sudden, vigorous, masculine fling, far down the side of the mountain.

"Oh," I cried, "I 'm so sorry it 's gone!"

Mr. Hamlin, who was busy cutting something on the remaining stick, gave me a look of quiet contempt.

"At least you are consistent," he said.

"Well," I ventured, after I had watched his carving for a moment, "you are inconsistent yourself. You thought it was impertinent for

Arthur Winthrop to make his initials without asking me, and now you are doing the same thing."

"That is entirely different," said Mr. Hamlin, with dignity.

"What is different?"

"The initials are different."

After this idiotic dialogue we gazed at each other a moment in silent disgust. Then we both laughed; after which we went down the mountain to a big pine, where I sat down to pin up the rents in my gown, and Mr. Hamlin carved whatever he chose upon my staff.

"I felt a little breeze," remarked Mr. Hamlin, intent upon his work.

I threw aside my hat, and a puff of cooler air lifted the hair on my forehead.

"How still it is!" I said.

The sun had gone behind a cloud, and the odors of hemlock and sweet fern had grown suddenly heavy.

" It 's a relief to have — " began Mr. Hamlin; then suddenly springing to his feet he exclaimed, " Look at that cloud ! "

Over the shoulder of the mountain was rising rapidly a cloud as dark as lead. The air became more breathless and oppressive than before, and a curious listening hush fell upon everything. In short, a heavy thunder-storm was close upon us.

" Oh, what shall we do? " I cried in great dismay. " How stupid of us to come so far ! We shall be drenched before we get back to the top and down the other side."

" We must go down this side," Mr. Hamlin decided promptly. " Give me your hand, Miss Betty; we must run for it."

Hand in hand, panting and breathless, we tore wildly down the mountain pasture, over sticks and stones, moss and rocky ledges, like a pair who were fleeing from fate. Mr. Hamlin's field-glass bumped against his hip as he ran, and my pail of berries swayed and swung. At every step the berries bobbed over the brim, and like Gretel, I left a trail behind me of scattered fruit. The first warm, slow drops of rain were beginning to fall when we reached the foot of the mountain; yet even here Mr. Hamlin would not let me stop, but, gasping that he saw a chimney, he hurried me across the pasture and down the dusty road. The rain was just upon us when we reached the Butterfield farm-house, and dashed recklessly in at the door, which stood hospitably open. Mr. Hamlin drew out a chair for me, but I sank into a heap on the floor. We were in a large, raftered kitchen, and the air was filled with the pleasant spicy odor of the wood fire, newly kindled in the stove. As we tumbled in at one door Mrs. Simeon Butterfield came in at another with an armful of sticks, which she threw down upon the floor.

"Wal," she said, in a rich, comfortable voice,

" hed a narrer squeak for 't, did n't ye? Little more 'n ye 'd been soppin'."

"We must beg your pardon," said Mr. Hamlin, " for coming in without knocking."

"Law sakes," said the woman, regarding us with a broad and friendly smile, "don't say a word; don't say a word. 'T want no time to stop for manners, I 'm sure."

She proceeded to fill her stove with wood, and opening the oven door, urged me to sit up and dry my boots.

"Ye 've about lost all your plums, I guess," she said sympathetically. "Adaline, she went over a spell ternoon and picked a mess for supper. I 'm a stewin' of 'em now in molasses. Adaline, she thinks there aint nothin' quite so good as her mar's stewed plums. Says she don't get nothin' like 'em over to the Corner."

While our hostess talked I had noticed a towzled, sandy head, which kept appearing at the door leading into the wood-house, and which dodged away as often as I looked.

"That's Elnathan," said the woman, apologetically. "I tell him folks might almost think he was n't well-witted, but he's only bashful. He's different from Adaline an' alwees was, though to be sure she's got a good many more manners than what she had before she went to the Corner. She's been down to the Corner two seasons, Adaline has, to work in the corn factory. I think them corn-factory folks are sort o' stuck up, and girls get high notions there."

She looked rather serious for a moment over Adaline's "high notions," then her face relapsed into its good-humored, easy expression.

"I guess ye must be from the Arrowsic camp, haint ye, over beyond the mounting? Elnathan, he's been over once to see ye. He's dretful curious about the camp an' tents, but after all he darsn't speak to them when he gets there,

he 's so dretful bashful. Good lands! Do look
at it rain ! "

The rain was indeed falling in sheets, but the
thunder and lightning were far off. It looked
almost as if it were settling down to storm all
night. Mr. Hamlin and I exchanged glances
of humorous despair. At this minute a door
opened, and the much-talked-of Adaline herself
appeared, surrounded by an admiring group of
children of assorted sizes.

She was a young girl, with a rather pretty,
silly face, and she had a self-conscious air which
her mother entirely lacked. She giggled and
shook her earrings about, as she looked at Mr.
Hamlin, and slid her wide black rubber brace-
lets up and down her wrists.

" This is my daughter Adaline," said our
hostess. " Adaline, this is Dr. Greenleaf's
daughter; don't you remember her? Rally,
though, I 've forgot what your name be," she
added, regarding Mr. Hamlin with a benevolent

look, "only seein' ye onct, ye know, when ye come with the medicine that day."

The name being given, and the ceremony of introduction concluded, our hostess ran on with her stream of talk.

"I always sot a sight by your father," she said, "an' I know him real well. He took our Eva May through the measles last winter; done it well, too. Now you must jest stop to supper; ye see it don't hold up a mite yet. Ef it haint done raining after supper, Elnath shall carry ye round home in the wagon. Now you go right into the fore-room, and Adaline will entertain ye. You play to 'em, Adaline, and show 'em the album, and I'll stir up somethin' for an early supper."

Reluctantly we agreed that it was quite impossible for us to start for home in such a storm, and though politely protesting against the supper, we yielded at length, and meekly followed Adaline into the " fore-room." The " fore-

room" was small and stuffy. It smelled of oil-
cloth and varnish and bombazine, but it was, of
its class, quite an opulent "fore-room." There
were a haircloth sofa and four slippery haircloth chairs. A mahogany centre-table was
covered with a white cloth with a knotted fringe.
In the middle stood a lamp on a green worsted
mat. Round about this were ranged the family
Bible, the album, a red pin-cushion made over
a broken goblet, and a box once covered with
shells pressed into putty, but now showing
chiefly the putty, with holes where the shells
had been. On the wall hung a hideous
"Death-bed of Abraham Lincoln," framed in
leather-work; a "Sailor's Return," in cones; a
Biblical scene, in pebbles; and a certificate of
membership of the M. E. American Mis-
sionary Society, enriched with a border of
beans.

Eva May, the smallest of the flock of children, not being at all afflicted with her brother

Elnathan's shyness, volunteered a good deal of information.

"That's Gran'f'ther Butterfield's coffin-plate," she said, pointing to a silver plate which adorned the wall above the mantel; "and that wreath in the frame, them was the flowers Aunt Silviny had onto her coffin. I went to her funiril," she added with awful relish. "That's the only funiril ever I ben to."

"Don't talk so much, Eva May Butterfield," said Adaline, setting forth two of the slippery chairs. "Do take seats."

We seated ourselves in silence. The atmosphere of the room was depressing, not to say funereal; and I longed for the old kitchen, with its cheerful mistress, its fragrant fire, and open door.

"Could n't we have the windows open?" suggested Mr. Hamlin.

"If you can get 'em open," said Adaline, dubiously. "They was stuck down when the house was painted, and they 've always stuck."

It proved that they stuck still; and after a brief but manful struggle, Mr. Hamlin gave it up, and we relapsed into gasping silence.

" I 'll show you the album, if you want to see it," said Adaline.

She openly addressed Mr. Hamlin, and established herself beside him. I had nothing to do but listen humbly from afar, and watch the rain.

"This," began Adaline, with the air of a show-man, "is Aunt Cath*rine*. She used to live over to Litchfield Corner, in a house with a bay window; she 's dead now. That 's Uncle Jeduthan, her husband; he 's dead, too. That 's my Aunt Adaline, that I was named for; she keeps three canaries. And that 's her first husband, Uncle John; he 's dead. Her second husband never was took; we aint got no picture of him."

"Why not?" asked Mr. Hamlin, briskly, rousing himself to take an interest in his entertainer's efforts, and frowning upon me as he detected me in a smile.

"Oh, he don't darse to," replied Adaline; "he 's too bashful. He 's dretful bashful, Uncle James is. That 's my cousin Julia; she 's dead now. That 's her twin brother, Jude; he 's joined the church this summer. That 's Aunt Samanthy; she 's dead. That 's mother's Uncle Peleg; his wife, she hung herself out in the barn, and Uncle Peleg, he never knew it; thought she 'd gone to some of the neighbors, till he went out to do the chores, and found her hanging in the tie-up."

"She was dead," cheerfully added Eva May, who stood by an interested listener.

"That," continued Adaline, "is Maria Carey; she 's gone to Idaho. That 's my brother four years ago."

"Is he dead?" asked Mr. Hamlin.

"Why, no," replied Adaline, much shocked, "that's Elnathan; did n't you see him out in the kitchen?"

I laughed gleefully though silently, and Mr. Hamlin shook his head at me over the elaborate plaits of Adaline's hair.

"Who is this queer-looking child with such big ears?" he asked.

"Oh, that's me when I was a baby," answered Adaline, slightly offended.

At this I laughed aloud, and after a minute Adaline decided to join me. We were still laughing when the door opened, and a young man was ushered in by Mrs. Butterfield.

"One more to keep ye company," she announced cheerfully. "Elnath had this young feller out in the barn. He came on one o' them crazy wheels that city boarders trapse about on now-days. You jest make yourselves to home, all of ye, and we'll hev supper in no time now."

The new-comer was a dark and rather handsome young man in brown velvet knickerbockers and a Norfolk jacket. He had evidently reached the shelter of the barn before the shower began, for he was as neat and jaunty as a fashion plate. He bowed slightly as Mrs. Butterfield presented him, and seating himself by the window became absorbed in studying the dripping lilac bush outside.

"I wisht you'd play me a tune," said Adaline, suddenly addressing me for the first time. "I wisht you would. I'm terrible fond of music."

"I cannot play," I replied, "but we should like to hear you."

"I don't play," answered Adaline, "I sing. But I haint practised for ever so long."

"Do sing," urged Mr. Hamlin. "Let me open the melodeon for you."

"Oh, I never should darst to," declared Adaline, nevertheless rising and following him. "I aint us't to singin' before strangers."

She sat down, however, with much giggling
and shaking of elbows. The chair proved to
be too low, and required a " Choral Wreath "
and a " Golden Lyre " to bring it up suffi-
ciently. Then, when she was fairly seated,
she was obliged to bend down half a dozen
times to be sure that the pedals were really
there.

" There, now ! " she exclaimed ; " I can't, and
I said I could n't."

"Oh, but you have n't tried yet," said Mr.
Hamlin, reassuringly. " Do try."

Thus coaxed and encouraged Adaline finally
yielded, and struck in boldly with that charming
ditty, " Pull for the Shore." Her voice was loud
and shrill. The pedals rattled and clattered, the
wind choked and gulped in the bellows ; but
Adaline, having started, sang on and on, paus-
ing neither for breath nor interlude, until she
had sung every verse, when she stopped panting,
saying meekly, —

"I haint sung any for a long time; I'm all hoarsed up."

Mrs. Butterfield had appeared at the door with floury hands, but a countenance beaming with placid approval.

"Sing 'em 'Surely the Captain May Depend on Me,'" she urged. "I call that about the handsomest tune of all."

Upon this Adaline obligingly began again. She not only sang her mother's favorite, but many others. She urged Mr. Hamlin to join in the chorus. I sat behind her and laughed at Mr. Hamlin, near-sightedly peering over Adaline's shoulder and singing Moody and Sankey favorites. The dark-faced young man looked melancholy, and gazed into the lilac bush. The rain had nearly stopped falling, and the blue sky was breaking through the clouds. I was about to suggest that we might safely start for home, when Eva May appeared at the door and announced supper.

The table was spread in the kitchen, and about the door leading into the wood-house several children were clustered, gazing longingly at the viands.

" Father 'n' Elnathan aint a comin'," announced one of them, shrilly. " Elnath says he druther eat in the tie-up than along of comp'ny."

" There, Victory, I guess that 'll do," said Mrs. Butterfield, with dignity. " You can come to table and set in Elnath's chair. See how much like a little lady you can act."

The sun had come out warm and bright, and shone in at the open kitchen door. In the pool of rain-water left in the hollow door-stone two gaunt, yellow-legged chickens disported themselves as we ate our supper.

" Ef I 'd only a 'known ye were comin'," said Mrs. Butterfield, hospitably, " I 'd a hed somethin' cooked up for ye; but, as 't is, I haint nothin' raly fit to set before comp'ny. I don't

know when I've hed sech awful poor luck with
my biscuits. Ef ye hed n't just come from
campin' out, I should be ashamed to offer 'em
to ye."

"Are you camping out?" asked the dark
young man, suddenly raising his eyes from his
plate.

Upon hearing that we were, he became unexpectedly interested in us. He was anxious to
know how we liked the life. He asked how we
employed our evenings, and what we did in
stormy weather. I thought he decidedly gave
Mr. Hamlin an opportunity to invite him to
visit the camp, but this, very naturally, Mr.
Hamlin did not do. The young man said that
he was spending some weeks at the "Gorge,"
a mountain village thirty miles above, where
summer visitors thronged.

"I am terribly afflicted with insomnia," fixing
his melancholy dark eyes upon my face. "My
physician has ordered me to spend much time

in the open air, and my bicycle and I have pretty thoroughly explored the country about here."

"You certainly cannot think of getting back to the Gorge to-night," said Mr. Hamlin, bluntly.

"Mrs. Butterfield has kindly promised me a bed for to-night," replied he, with a smile. "I believe I will take a little spin for exercise, if the roads will allow it."

We had left the table and were standing grouped about the open door.

"We must be getting home at once," said Mr. Hamlin, decidedly; "your sister will be anxious about you, Miss Betty."

The dark young man had disappeared, and now returned rolling beside him a bicycle, whose great wheel looked as though a big spider had spun it. Mr. Hamlin went forward to examine the beautiful machine, and I tried to thank our hostess for her kindness.

"Don't say a word, now, don't say a word,"

she said; "'t was pot-luck, and poor enough at that. You're real welcome, I'm sure. Lands! Do see him; he's histin' himself up."

The dark young man had mounted his bicycle, and was running up and down before the house for the benefit of the children, who stood staring in open-mouthed wonder. From the door of the barn the bashful Elnathan and his frowzy-haired father looked on with much interest.

"Gosh!" exclaimed Elnathan, admiringly, "I sh'd like to try that myself. Looks dretful easy."

"Ye great loon," replied his father, "ye couldn't no more ride it than ye could ride our young bull."

As we started for the camp along the wet road, the bicycler joined us.

"If you wouldn't mind," he said, gracefully touching his Tam-o'-Shanter cap, "I should very much like to ride a little distance with you."

"Certainly," said Mr. Hamlin, not very cordially; and the three of us soon left behind the hospitable house of the Butterfields, and the staring group about the door. The sun was not yet set, and the air was full of fresh wild odors of brake and pine and moss. When we passed through the little beech wood-road the drops of rain were still pattering softly among the dripping leaves, and now and then falling, slow and heavy, to the already sodden earth. The frogs were croaking in a noisy chorus, glad of the rain; and deep among the trees, a wood bird was calling in a voice of delicious sweetness.

Just beyond the wood our escort said goodnight and left us. I turned and watched him as he rode away. He looked a very handsome young figure in his velvet clothes and dark-red cap.

"What a very good-looking young man!" I exclaimed.

"Yes," assented Mr. Hamlin, whipping the drenched roadside bushes with my alpenstock, "he's good enough looking, but his get-up is confoundedly theatrical."

"He looks melancholy," I said sentimentally, "as if he had some trouble weighing on him."

"Dyspepsia," returned Mr. Hamlin, briefly, still whipping the bushes.

"You *couldn't* have seen him eat ham and hot soda biscuit," I laughed, "if you think that."

It was three miles round the mountain road, and it was quite dark when at last we reached Sippican Meadow and saw the fire burning below the tents. We found the camp in a damp and discouraged condition. They were gathered in the dining tent attempting to tell stories. They had supped upon cheese and limp crackers, and, altogether, it seemed that our lot had been happier than theirs.

"Josephine is angry," whispered Lucretia to

me as we were going to bed. "You know she thinks Mr. Hamlin is her property. And it really was improper, too," she added; "I don't know, I'm sure, what Aunt Jane would say."

Miss Alexander came across to me presently, with her wavy red hair hanging below her waist and her eyes shining like stars. She looked almost pretty. She brought a box of chocolates, and offered them to me as I sat on the edge of my bed.

"Don't you like them? They are Maillard's," she said. "I would n't stir from home without a supply of Maillard's confectionery. Are n't you dreadfully tired?"

"Oh, no," I replied cheerfully. "I am so strong. I'm a country girl, you know. It was really quite a funny adventure."

"I wish I had been there," she said suddenly. Then she fell to studying her pretty, delicate hands. "How demoralizing camp life is," she mused. "I use my *toilette des ongles* every day, yet my fingers are growing hideous. I should be ashamed to have anybody kiss my hand now."

"I should at any time," I said bluntly. "I should feel like an idiot."

Miss Alexander gave me an enthusiastic, sudden squeeze.

"What a dear little innocent daisy you are!" she exclaimed. "I should like to confide in you."

"You 'd better not," I returned; "I always tell things."

"Was your sister scolding you for coming home alone with Mr. Hamlin?" she asked. "To be sure, though, you were n't alone, for the young bicycler escorted you."

"Only a little way," I said. "He went back to Mrs. Butterfield's to spend the night. I think he is going back to the Gorge to-morrow. He wore a beautiful brown velvet suit. I wish all the young men were dressed that way."

" Brown velvet is very becoming to those light men," observed Miss Alexander.

" He was not light," I corrected. " He was very dark, and he looked very grave and melancholy. I quite pitied him."

" You are a darling!" exclaimed Miss Alexander, with another hug. " You may keep the chocolates. Good-night, *chérie.*"

XV.

WHAT BOB SAYS.

You see this bow-and-arrow business would be all well enough if you ever hit anything; but the plain truth is that you don't. Here we've been over two weeks in camp, and not one single confounded thing has anybody shot. Of course the boiled ham and beef that we brought along with us lasted a few days, but since we finished that, we've just lived on fish till I wonder we don't have fins grow. This is n't half as jolly a camping-out as last year. We had plenty to eat then. Betty is different too. She's all gone to pieces; no fun in her. She has n't been fishing with Fred and me half the time.

Yesterday Fred and I went for pickerel over to Mason's Pond, on the road to the Gorge, and when we'd most got there we met a fellow on a bicycle. It was a boss one. I never saw such a good one in my life. He rode boss, too. He could stand still on it, almost. Fred and I stopped to watch him, and he got off to fix something, so we got to talking with him, and that's how he came to give me the letter. It was to Miss Alexander. Betty does n't like her, but I think she's a first-rate sort of a girl.

She has had a hard time of it at home, too, I guess, but she is n't afraid of spiders; so the fellow said if I 'd give her the note, and not let anybody see, he 'd be awfully obliged. You see, we 'd told him about ourselves and the camp, and then he offered me a ride. I did try it, too, it looked so easy. Fred just climbed up and keeled over, and I did n't stay on quite as long as Fred. So, of course, I did give her the note, and as —

There 's Fred, and we 're going across the pond for sweet flag.

XVI.

WHAT BETTY SAYS.

"MR. HAMLIN," called Mrs. Sparhawk, pleasantly, "Miss Alexander and I are going to the Glen. Will you not come with us to protect us from wild beasts?"

We all looked up in some surprise. It was a perfect morning, with a cool breeze darkening the surface of the pond; but Mrs. Sparhawk was by no means fond of walking over country roads, and usually preferred remaining behind in her hammock, to joining any of our expeditions. Mr. Hamlin rose from the grass and brushed the cigar ashes from his blue flannel garments.

"By all means," he said, not very cordially. "Why don't we all go?"

Nobody else appeared to wish to start, however. Mrs. Winthrop had cooking to do; Mrs. Dudley considered the Glen a damp and rheumatic spot; Emily wished to see if she could not finish her chair-cover that morning, and Lucretia, Josephine, Ted, and Arthur Winthrop had ensconced themselves under the shade of the apple-tree, too comfortably to be disturbed.

I should have liked to go myself, and was about to say so, when Mrs. Sparhawk asked me to take care of the children.

"You are so good-natured, Miss Betty," she said, "that I fear I'm imposing on you, but the Colonel will soon be through with his letters, and then you can turn the young imps over to him. Are you ready, Annie?"

Annie Alexander rose from her camp-chair rather languidly. She had told me one evening that she had a hidden grief, but I thought myself that she must get a good deal of consolation from her gowns. She is one of those people with a positive genius for dress.

Josephine looks like a commonplace dowdy beside her. Nothing could be simpler than her gray batiste gown and her little black hat; and yet there was nobody in camp to compare with her, as she unfurled her large batiste sun-umbrella and stepped off beside Mr. Hamlin.

"There goes a thoroughly artificial girl," commented Mrs. Winthrop, unwisely, "and yet every man in the camp is fascinated by her."

"*What* did you say was the matter with her?" asked Rodney Sparhawk, shrewdly. "She gives me choclits, and Bevis stole my sugared almond."

"Did n't civer, stoled it yousef," promptly responded the warlike Bevis, digging so violently with an iron spoon that the sand flew in our eyes.

"I think he has forgotten what you said," I said softly to Mrs. Winthrop. "He could not understand your words."

" I 'm goin' in bavin'," announced Bevis. " Tired o' diggin' dirt."

" Wait until Papa comes, Bevis," I urged. " I do not think he would like you to go in so soon after breakfast."

" He wants me to be clean," put in Rodney, " so I guess we better go right off. We always did at home."

" Why, Rodney," I said, trying by discussion to divert them from really going in, " you have no pond at home."

" We bathed in the cistern," replied Rodney, with dignity. " Now I think we better take off our stockings to save time, and take off our shoes too."

" What is going on here, pray, you nasty little apes ? " asked a fond maternal voice, and Mrs. Sparhawk appeared beside us.

She took a seat, adjusted her glasses, and began to fan herself.

" I could not endure it, after all," she said

plaintively. "I did want to see the cascade, and I thought the Glen would be so deliciously cool; but that dreadful country road was too bad. Really, my ankles are quite twisted out of joint. I had to give it up and come back."

"And the others went on?" asked Mrs. Winthrop.

"Yes," replied Mrs. Sparhawk, smiling. "Mr. Hamlin urged poor Annie so that she really could n't refuse."

She fanned herself slowly for a moment, and then added, —

"Quite a case of infatuation. Annie *is* one of the most infatuating creatures! She always takes men by storm."

"Do you want the children to go in bathing, Mrs. Sparhawk?" I asked abruptly. "They said they were going, but I thought it was too near their breakfast time."

"And you were right, you real little doctor's

daughter," she said gayly. "Children, you are absolutely not to go into the water, not one step, do you understand?"

"We've got our shoes and stockings all off," said Rodney.

"Very well, put them on again," said Mrs. Sparhawk, with fine decision.

She picked up her French novel from the grass and began to read, while the children calmly and happily proceeded to go in wading. As nobody else appeared to pay the slightest attention to the little things, I went down to the beach beside them, where my own gown speedily became quite drabbled and spattered from the children's splashing.

"Here comes a horse-car," announced Rodney, unexpectedly.

Horse-cars not running regularly over the Sippican Mountain route, Rodney's remark met with more than usual attention. I looked up, and Emily Dudley put down her embroidery.

"It is Mrs. Jarley," said Arthur Winthrop, from his seat under the tree.

"It is Dr. Marigold," declared Colonel Sparhawk, who had just come out of the dining tent.

"A circus! a circus!" cried Bevis, spattering wildly out of the water. "Come quick, Papa, and wipe my two feets. The grass is pricky."

"I'll tell you," exclaimed Ted, springing from the ground; "it is a travelling photographer."

"What fun!" joined in Josephine; "now we'll all have our pictures taken."

The van was gayly painted with red, and had a white funnel running out of one end. A little glass roof rose in the middle. The car was drawn by two bony horses, and the reins extended directly into the open door. The driver was invisible.

With one accord we abandoned books and work and hastened up the meadow. Even Mrs. Sparhawk strolled after us, adjusting her eyeglass, and declaring that this was "really very droll, you know."

"Hi!" shouted Ted. "Stop! Don't go by."

He need not have been afraid of this, as it proved, for by the time we reached the road the car had stopped. A young man in a gingham coat came out, followed by a red-haired boy, and began to unharness the travel-tired horses.

"How de do?" asked the gingham-coated one, politely. "Dry spell we've ben havin' lately."

He went on briskly with his work while we all stood and stared at him, much as a band of natives might have stared at Stanley in the trackless wilds of Africa.

"Turn 'em out, Harmon, and let 'em feed down along the road," said the master of the caravan to the boy.

He let down a small flight of steps from the end of the car.

"Now, ladies and gents," he said politely, "walk right in and make yourselves to home. I heard about the camp over to Snow's Falls, and I drove down this mornin' a purpose to 'commodate you."

"That was very kind of you," observed Ted, slyly.

"I'm always glad to 'commodate," the man replied. "I thought like enough you'd like a chance to set. Walk in and look at the pictures, anyway, even if you should n't wish to be took. Walk right in. Don't be bashful."

Thus invited, we all clambered into the car, Rodney and Bevis making themselves, as Theodore remarked, "rather too frequent," and nearly knocking over the rest of us in their haste to be first in the field.

"I mus' have my picksher took," cried Bevis, shrilly. "Rodney had his las' winter, and he cried an' then he had candy."

"That was a tooth, you silly little boy," said

Rodney, with a superior air; " and I guess you 'd
have cried 'bout that."

Within the car the atmosphere was stuffy and
smelled of chemicals. The glass roof had a
curtain of faded blue cambric. There was a
sort of screen at the further end, a couple of
steamer-like berths, a cupboard, a little rusty
stove, a few chairs, and a table on which were
the untidy remnants of a meal. In cases hanging
against the wall were the pictures: tintypes of
every size, from minettes at twenty-five cents a
dozen, to the imposing " Emperial Bodoor," —
" a French name," the photographer explained
casually and condescendingly, — which were half
a dollar apiece. He added, to take the sting
from this exorbitant price, that they were as
much sought after as real oil painting, and
" would wear better, besides."

We found the pictures more entertaining than
the proprietor, and spent some time in exam-
ining them. There were farmers and farmers'

wives, rustic beaux and belles, and family groups of children. Some were simpering, and some wore an expression of wide-eyed horror, as if they were in momentary expectation of the camera's exploding like a dynamite bomb. Nearly every girl grasped a bouquet firmly. It was always the same bouquet, and we easily recognized the original in the bunch of faded pink muslin roses lying upon a chair. As for the men, they mostly sat in ox-eyed blankness. The large right hand clutched an unaccustomed book; the left hand was carelessly disposed upon the knee. There was, too, in nearly every picture a bit of rustic stump in some position in foreground or background.

"Now," announced cheerful Mr. Winthrop at last, taking pity upon the wistful artist, — "now we must all have pictures. Who sits first?"

"Me!" shouted Rodney and Bevis in shrill chorus.

And in fact they were taken at once, "the

better," as their mother remarked, "to have the nasty, troublesome little creatures out of the way."

Mrs. Dudley from the steps without urged her daughter to leave the car.

"Emily," she said plaintively, "if you will persist in staying, at least come here and let me wet your handkerchief in camphor. Those chemicals must be bad to breathe."

"I see," said Colonel Sparhawk, "that you have a rustic stump. Do you charge more for introducing that?"

"Not a cent more," replied the artist, "though I dare say some would. I don't mind saying that it's a second-handed stump, though you would n't think it. It is every bit as genteel as what it ever was. I got it at a bargain of Perkins Brothers over to Reedville, though, as 't was, I paid a good high price for it too. Perkins Brothers, they'd had it a considerable spell, and their patrons had all ben took with it, so they planned for somethin' new and taking. Amos, the oldest, he was for having a trellis; but Andrew, he was sot on a post with an urn atop of it. I never knew which they got at last, but I bought the stump, and it's brought me in more setters than you'd believe."

"What exciting things have taken place in our absence!" cried a gay voice at the door.

"I firmly believe, Mrs. Sparhawk," chimed in the voice of Mr. Hamlin, "that you knew of this by second-sight, and tried to cheat us out of having our pictures taken."

"Indeed, I did not," protested Mrs. Sparhawk, laughing. "In proof of my fairness, see, you shall have the next sitting. Let us have a group,—Miss Alexander seated on the stump, and you standing gracefully beside her."

"I detest having my picture taken; let us off, please," begged Miss Alexander, prettily.

"No," laughed Mrs. Sparhawk; "really, I am

inflexible.   To please me, Annie.   You know I
have a fancy for my own way."

"*Ipsa dixit*," murmured the Colonel, with a
grimace.   "If I had chanced to say that!"

Somehow all the fun seemed to have gone
out of the thing since Mr. Hamlin came.   I felt
cross and out of patience with Bevis and Rodney,
and the whole affair of the picture-taking grew
as stupid as possible.   Miss Alexander con-
sented, after much urging, to sit on the stump;
and after she and Mr. Hamlin were taken, Mrs.
Winthrop and Bevis had a picture.   Then
Mr. Winthrop, holding that absurd bouquet;
then Mrs. Sparhawk, with the stump in the
foreground; Bob and Fred in fishing cos-
tume, with the stump between them; Emily,
Josephine, and Lucretia, with the stump dimly
seem in the background; Theodore, Emily,
and Lucretia; Arthur Winthrop with his geo-
logical hammer; and in nearly every picture
Rodney and Bevis, with many heads and hands,

because keeping still was with them an utter impossibility.

" You have n't had your picture taken, Betty," said Bob, most inopportunely.

" I 'm not going to," I answered, preparing to leave the car.

Almost everybody had gone back to the camp. Only the children and the two boys were left.

" Do have it taken, just for fun," urged Bob. " All the rest of us have."

" Do," added Bevis; " and me too, I 'll be tooken."

" Bevis, dear," said Miss Alexander from the door, " Papa is going out in the boat with Rodney, and wants you to come too."

" What is this about your picture? " asked Mr. Hamlin, coming in. " Have you had the big one taken yet? "

" What big one? " I asked.

" Why, the 'Emperial Bodoor' for your father."

" Father detests tintypes," I said.

" For your Aunt Jane, then, or for Harriet; no matter for whom. You are to sit on the stump and hold your sailor hat in your lap — *s'il vous plait.*"

" But it does not," I cried, vexed; " I do not wish to be taken at all."

" Don't be a gump, Bet," advised Bob. " What do you want to be so silly for? Go ahead."

" Emperial Bodoor, sir?" asked the artist, bustling about and disregarding me entirely.

" I shall look as disagreeable as I possibly can," I announced crossly, as I seated myself.

" You 'd better not trouble yourself," said Bob, frankly, " for you 're a regular guy anyway, with your hair like a rat's nest and your collar crooked."

" Never mind," I said, when at last the sitting was through; " I shall give it to Harriet, and she won't mind."

After supper we sat on the rugs before the tents, while Arthur Winthrop and Theodore tried to give us a burlesque of the ghost scene in Hamlet. It was not very funny, and we had to try very hard to laugh at all. Perhaps we might have found it more amusing if the actors had found it less so.

Mr. Hamlin came down the field after a time with our pictures. They were protected with little curtains of magenta paper. After we had gazed upon the tintypes we were thankful for the curtains.

"They are hideous," said Mrs. Sparhawk. "Limkin, dear, crunch mine up."

"My life," said the Colonel, "let me keep one, at least."

"Not one; they are libellous," declared his wife.

"Oh, my shoul," piped Bevis, who was making himself quite detestable with his unhampered criticisms. "Do look! Miss Betty's got a nawful big one, — bigger 'n any uvver body's here."

" Why, Betty," said Lucretia, " how very funny for you to have such a big one ! "

" I hate a lot of little ones always round in my button-box," I said.

" You must have had it taken on purpose for some one person, I should think," said Josephine, laughing slyly.

" She did," said Bobby, coming to the rescue ; " she had it taken for Harriet Tuell."

" It was my fault," said Mr. Hamlin ; " I advised it."

" Mr. Hamlin," said Mrs. Sparhawk, " the dew is falling ; will you please take this wrap across to Miss Alexander, and give her a gentle scolding for trying to write in this half-light ? "

The car had already been hitched to its horses and started on its homeward way. Rodney and Bevis were borne away to bed by their father.

Miss Alexander and Mr. Hamlin strolled to and fro on the little beach. Ted and Arthur were singing college songs. Presently, when it was darker and damper, the camp-fire was lighted. Mr. Hamlin and Miss Alexander came and joined us. She looked almost like a beauty with Mrs. Sparhawk's silvery chuddah arranged in the Egyptian fashion about her head. I wondered how I ever could have thought her plain. I thought it was no wonder Mr. Hamlin liked her.

" Oh, look ! " I cried suddenly. " A will-o'-the-wisp."

A round ball of yellow light moved swiftly along the crest of the meadow and vanished.

" Where? " asked several voices. " What was it? "

A hand clasped mine convulsively.

" For Heaven's sake do not say any more ! " murmured the voice of Miss Alexander in my ear. " *Do not. You may ruin me.*"

"It was a meteor," I said inanely.

But I withdrew my hand from Miss Alexander's clasp, and in a moment, to get away from her, I pleaded a headache and went to bed.

XVII.

WHAT BOB SAYS.

WHAT 's a fellow to do when a girl asks him, even if he does n't want to do it ? When she came and cried, and said how she felt; said I was the only real friend she had in camp; said she could trust me, and all the time, you know, kept on crying like anything, — of course, I took the note and carried it to him.

He turned out to be the bicycle fellow. I thought so when I saw the light sail by. I tell you what, though, it is a boss bicycle; a Columbia. It is even more stunning than I thought that day. He said if we 'd come over to-morrow we might try it all the morning. Asked me if I 'd tell her just " waiting; " that one word. So I did.

In the night it rained, and the waterproof tent leaked, and the flour barrel is full of paste this morning. We had crackers and boiled eggs for breakfast. No meat for two weeks. To-day we must begin shooting in dead earnest; no more fooling.

XVIII.

WHAT BETTY SAYS.

EVERY morning Emily Dudley, who always tries to do her duty, takes her bow and goes up the road to the beech-wood shooting. She never has shot anything; in fact, there's nothing to shoot but squirrels and woodchucks, but she still perseveres in the most admirable manner.

Perhaps living upon bread and milk and fruit is depressing. At any rate we are growing stupid at Camp Sippican. Yesterday morning Mrs. Sparhawk actually threatened to go home unless we made an effort to be entertaining.

"I do not care for myself, you know," she said amiably, "but Annie Alexander is my guest, and it is my duty to make her visit pleasant. Mr. Hamlin, do please go and ask her to play backgammon. She is moping over a book in the dining tent."

Mr. Hamlin, who was playing cat's cradle with Rodney, rose obediently and departed. He is always very happy to wait on Mrs. Sparhawk. In a few minutes he returned with Miss Alexander and the backgammon board. Miss Alexander looked pale and jaded, in spite of her bewitching toque and jacket of blue cloth and silver braids. She sat down upon the grass hopelessly.

"I am in a most abominable temper," she declared. " You much better have left me alone, Mr. Hamlin."

" Everybody is in a nasty temper this morning," said Mrs. Sparhawk. "I wonder why."

"It is the change in the weather," replied Mrs. Dudley, solemnly. " I woke *shivering* at three o'clock this morning. I am quite positive we shall all be ill, and no doctor."

" Betty can doctor you," spoke up Bob, who

sat near getting his fish-lines in order. "Betty doctored me once when Father and Aunt Jane were away, and I had a diphtheretic throat. She set Ned's leg once, too. Just as good as ever now, is n't it, Neddy?"

Ned, lying near in his favorite flattened position, opened his eyes and thumped in a perfunctory manner on the ground with his tail. Mr. Hamlin gave me an odd, quick look; and Josephine said, —

"How funny for a girl to set a dog's leg! I never could have done it, I am so tender-hearted."

"It is a pity all women are not tender-hearted," said Mr. Hamlin, grimly.

"I am going up to the farm," announced pleasant Mrs. Winthrop, coming out with her hands full of parcels. "I am going to make blueberry pies and gingerbread. Who will come up and help me carry my things?"

"I will," I cried, jumping up, glad of something to do.

"I will come and help with the pies in ten minutes," called Mrs. Dudley from her mending.

"I 'll take the flour-bucket," said Fred, good-naturedly, leaving his game of solitaire to follow us across the field.

The farm which supplies us with milk and vegetables is only a short distance beyond the turn of the road, and here we have hired the occasional use of a "back kitchen" and a stove for such cooking as cannot be done well at camp. Having seen Mrs. Winthrop, as Harriet would say, "in the middle of the pies," Fred rode triumphantly off on the farmer's mowing-machine, while I loitered under a wide-spreading butternut-tree beyond the farm-house. It was a perfect morning, clear and cool, and a fresh little breeze sent the wheat rippling and bending in the sunny field across the road. I sat down on a stone and took off my hat. I saw no special reason for hurrying back to camp. I made myself very comfortable, and was wishing for something to read, when round the bend of the road came Mr. Hamlin. Miss Alexander was not with him, and he was walking quickly.

"I concluded you were not coming back," he called out.

"I've been gone about fifteen minutes," I said, trying to look dignified. "I suppose I have a right to stay as long as I choose."

"Oh, no, you have not," said Mr. Hamlin, cheerfully.

He sat down uninvited, and began to twirl his gray Tam-o'-Shanter on the end of his walking-stick.

"I wish you would n't do that," I said crossly; "you make me dizzy."

Mr. Hamlin stopped promptly.

"Are you out of temper?" he asked cheerfully, "or only hungry?"

"I certainly am not cross," I replied frigidly.

"What is the matter then?" he asked, regarding me frankly.

I could hardly tell him, what I was forced to

own to myself, that I was cross because he had been playing backgammon with Miss Alexander. I preserved a solemn silence.

"I'll tell you what let's do," said Mr. Hamlin, boyishly; "let's run away!"

"What do you mean?" I asked severely.

"Oh, nothing," he said, and shied a stone at a tiny chipmunk which darted like a brown flash along the stone wall opposite.

Presently he stepped to an apple-tree near by, and cutting a branch, began to trim it for whittling.

"Sh'll tell Father," said a shrill and unexpected voice behind us; and turning, we discovered Tommy Durgin, the small son of the farmer, standing watching our movements with the utmost suspicion.

"Sh'll tell Father," he repeated threateningly.

"Tell him what?" asked Mr. Hamlin.

"Sh'll tell him ye went 'n cut a bough off'n the hightop tree."

"Well, I would," said Mr. Hamlin, continuing his whittling with much calmness. "And since you are going, I would go at once. Don't let us detain you."

"Huh?" said the boy, bewildered.

He stared vacantly at us for a moment. He did not understand Mr. Hamlin's words, but he did realize that he was being "made fun of," and his smouldering wrath arose.

"Set the dog on yer!" he cried.

"Oh, I think not," said Mr. Hamlin, unmoved. "You see, Tommy, the dog has gone to the hay-field with your father."

Angry and baffled, the boy stood looking at us with evil eyes, and shoving the loose sand back and forth with his leathery left foot. I knew his dull wit was striving to produce some new and withering speech, and I wondered what it would be. It came soon enough.

"Is that your girl?" he asked, grinning fiendishly. "Homelier 'n a stump fence!"

At this unexpected turning of the batteries on me, Mr. Hamlin darted suddenly forward, the boy flying like a dry leaf before him, while I hastened along the road in the other direction. In a moment Mr. Hamlin joined me, rather out of breath. I did not speak, and for some moments we walked on in silence.

"I gave that imp of darkness as thorough a shaking-up as ever he had in his life, I flatter myself," said Mr. Hamlin at last.

"He is a horrible child," I said vehemently; "*how* I hate him!"

Again we trudged along the dusty road in silence.

"When we get to the circus —" began Mr. Hamlin, casually.

"What circus?" I demanded, stopping short in the road.

"The circus at Snow's Falls," he replied. "I supposed that was where you were going, so I thought I'd go too."

"Of course you knew I was not," I replied. "I was not going anywhere, only away from that dreadful boy. Let us turn back."

"No," he persisted, "we are going to the circus."

"I never went to a circus in my life," I said, smiling with pure pleasure and dallying with temptation.

"You shall not say that to-night," he said easily.

"Oh, I can't go," I decided virtuously; "Lucretia would not like it. Aunt Jane disapproves of the circus. I always fancied it must be nice for that reason. But I must not go."

"That is nonsense," exclaimed Mr. Hamlin, decidedly.

He likes his own way. I do not think he cared a whit about my going, in the first place, but because I resisted he was at once determined that I should go.

"There is no reason at all that you should not go. It will be a regular lark. I'll tell

Lucretia it was all my fault. Here, I'll give you three minutes to decide; but remember now, Miss Betty, I shall not respect you at all unless you go."

His manner angered me, and I turned and walked resolutely away. When I had been walking for what seemed to me ten minutes, I glanced over my shoulder. Then I was lost. My good resolution faded. I retraced my steps shamefacedly.

" You ought not to make it so hard for me," I said pathetically.

" One minute," he replied.

" You are unkind," I declared. " I think you ought to urge me to go back instead — "

" Half a minute," he said.

" Oh," I cried desperately, " I will go, but I know I shall be sorry."

" Good child," he said, closing his watch with a snap.

I knew that I was not good; but having once

decided to follow my evil inclinations, I determined not to make myself unhappy by thinking
of consequences, and we started off quite merrily
upon our three-mile walk. To tell the truth, I
was decidedly flattered that Mr. Jack Hamlin
should care to ask me to go anywhere with him.
He always asks Lucretia, unless he is managed
by Mrs. Sparhawk, and then he escorts Miss
Alexander. As for me, I am generally left to
the company of Bobby and Fred. I suppose,
however, that Mr. Hamlin's invitation need not
have flattered me, for, as Lucretia said this
morning, " of course he would never have dared
invite Miss Alexander to so vulgar an entertainment as a circus."

After we passed the spot where the road
branched to run around the mountain, we began
to come upon the country people bound, like
ourselves, for the circus. Some were walking,
but many had come from the hill farms and
rode in shabby wagons, whole families together,

bent stolidly upon enjoying themselves. They
did not look merry at all, but regarded us with
dull and vacant eyes. They carried their dinners packed in wooden boxes painted green or
blue, and were prepared to thoroughly " see the
circus " from beginning to end.

As we walked on, the sun rode higher and the
breeze fell away. The dust from the passing
wagons was stifling. Very often we had offers
from the kindly drivers: " Pick ye up? " or
" Give ye a lift? " but these were refused. Mr.
Hamlin was in high spirits, and pretending to
be a showman, set forth in absurdly extravagant
terms the attractions of the circus.

" Only think," he added, " I should not have
known there was any circus except for Miss
Alexander. She knew. Miss Alexander is a
most mysterious person. How do you fancy
she found out? "

" I 've given up fancying things about Miss
Alexander," I replied, rather ill-temperedly.

I could not decently explain to Mr. Hamlin that I believed Miss Alexander to be a humbug, who tried to be strange and odd, just to attract attention.

"Hark!" said Mr. Hamlin; "we must be very near the falls. How loud they sound!"

In fact, we were much nearer than we thought. We were then in a deliciously cool and shady bit of maple wood, and as the trees became less crowded, we caught through the trunks the gleaming rush of the falls, and felt a cool mist from the chasm which yawned below. Beyond the road in a broad meadow shone the white tents of the circus, and on the other side of the river the village of Snow's Falls, perched on the ragged side of the gorge. We scrambled eagerly down the chasm until we reached a spot where broad stones were shaded by the trees, which further up hung desperately to the side of the cliff, with half their roots exposed. We rested and became peaceful, while I cooled my face

and hands in the clear brown water, and Mr.
Hamlin made a hasty sketch of the old Indian
Rock, under which, behind the veil of falling
water, a party of white settlers had once shel-
tered themselves and avoided massacre. There
was nothing down here but coolness and peace
and the sound of the water; and we were nearly
forgetting the object of our visit, when, from
above, a harsh and strident voice like a steam-
whistle began to shriek out a tune in the sem-
blance of the "Guards' Waltz."

"What is that?" I said, startled.

"That," replied Mr. Hamlin, rising promptly
and offering me a helping hand, "is the voice
of the far-famed calliope, — the 'only perfect
imitation of the human voice known to science.'
It reminds me that we are forgetting the circus.
If we do not hurry, we shall not have time for
half the side-shows."

"We are not going to the side-shows?" I
said incredulously.

" Every one," replied Mr. Hamlin, as we scrambled up the bank. " I shall spare you nothing, Miss Betty."

I could not tell always whether Mr. Hamlin were in earnest or in fun, but I soon found that he was in earnest in this. One or two real horrors he did indeed spare me, but for the rest we dutifully visited every booth and tent, and reached the circus proper in the most absurd state of childish laughter and idiocy.

To tell the truth, it was not much of a circus. At any rate, Mr. Hamlin made fun of it, but I confess that I took a sneaking delight in everything. Mr. Hamlin declared that the lions were stuffed and the dromedaries moth-eaten. He jeered at the poor old tiger, and advised the elephant to buy a rubber blanket and make himself a new cover.

" Look ! " he exclaimed, with sudden glee; " there are Adaline and the bicycle fellow, over by the dromedaries."

I was just looking to behold this wonder, when I was suddenly greeted by a rich, good-humored voice behind us.

"Why, how de do? Who 'd 'a' thought now o' your comin' to circus! Haint this a good joke, our meetin' of you?"

It was Mrs. Butterfield, fat and jovial, with all her numerous family straggling after her, from the greatest to the least. She was warm and ruddy and panting. She wore a gown of green and black plaids, and an ample *visite* of thin, shiny black silk. A wide collar, fastened by a pin containing hair, had slipped around until the brooch was under her left ear. Her hair was coming unfastened, and one auburn lock had fallen down her back from under her bonnet. With her vigorous right elbow she was valiantly forcing her way through the crowd, while her left hand, enclosed in a black silk mitt, grasped the wrist of Hiram Butterfield. The rest of the children followed like bobs to a kite-tail.

"Wal," she said, "who would 'a' thought of seein' you to circus! Mr. Dexter's here, too. He's just took Adaline to see the beasts. Ye know he's ben stoppin' to our house a spell. He says on 'count o' the view, though I never did think we lived in a very stylish place, sot on by the mountains as we be. He rides all day and evenin's, too; we don't see much of him. He don't make no trouble at all."

"What sort of a crank do you take him for?" muttered Mr. Hamlin in my ear.

"We're goin' to make a day of it," continued Mrs. Butterfield. "Started out at five o'clock this mornin' so's to git here in season to see circus come in. Goin' to stop to the evenin' show and spend the night at his brother Elnathan's, at the Falls. Land o' Goshen!" she added, with her easy chuckle; "did ye ever see the beat of this crowd? It doos seem as if we should n't never git sight o' them monkeys. Almiry, you jest hang holt of Eva May, now."

She stopped, and failing of the monkeys, drew up her line before the den of the unhappy polar bear.

"Wal," she remarked, "you don't look not to say sociable. How do ye like bein' kep' on ice?"

The great bear regarded her viciously from his sulky red eyes, but did not cease for a moment the restless swinging from side to side of his small head. He did not appear to be strongly reminded of his polar home by the presence in his cage of a piece of ice about large enough for a water-cooler.

"Don't he look terrible ugly though?" asked Mrs. Butterfield. "Lands! I'm glad I aint his keeper. Did I tell ye what a time we had gittin' here? Wagon broke down just after we got apast the Turner Road. 'T was broke last cattle-fair time, but he'd sort o' mended of it up somehow with a piece o' rope, and said he guessed 't would hold; but this load was a leetle too much for it, and down we went, I tell ye. He 'd to untackle and hide the team behind the alder bushes in Harskill's medder. We 'd to foot it into the village, him a leadin' of old Lucy."

She laughed at the recollection, and fanned herself with a " Short History of the Life of the Living Skeleton, including some of his Songs and gests."

" What a beastly crowd!" Mr. Hamlin said, successfully defending me from a pointed parasol which was prodding wildly and vindictively about in the throng to clear a passage for its owner into the now closely packed circus tent.

" My good woman, be careful, if you please. You almost hit this young lady in the face."

" Don't call me your ' good woman,'" said an acid female voice. " I 've earned and paid for my own ticket to this show. I aint nowise beholden to nobody, and I 'm agoin' to git in, and hev as good a seat as the next one, too, or my name aint Lizy Doble."

As she gave a final vigorous punch with her sunshade and was engulfed in the crowd, Mrs. Butterfield gave a tolerant laugh.

"Poor Lizy Ann," she said; "she don't hev no one to look out for her. The poor critter's alwers had a hard time of it, fendin' for herself, and she jest goes through life with all her sharp corners stickin' out to purtect herself. What's the matter with Eva May?" she added, looking back along the straggling line of Butterfields to where the wailing Eva May brought up the rear.

"She wants to see the Hairy Girl," piped Andrew Jackson across the crowd.

"Tut, tut!" exclaimed Mrs. Butterfield, in mellow tones of reproach. "Why, now, Eva May, I'm real mortified at ye. Anybody'd think a little gell that had seen a double-headed calf an' an Injy-rubber man an' a nice living skeleton all in one day had ought to be satisfied. An' there 's Father gone off to buy somethin' nice to eat; an' here 's Lysander goin' to wait by the tent door a purpose to catch him an' bring him where we 're a settin'."

Eva May being by this time brought to the front, tear-stained and dishevelled, her mother stopped, regardless of the elbowing throng about her, to wipe the child's wet face and twitch down her pink calico frock.

"There," she said, "now be a good gell an' stop your crying. Don't ye give one more sithe. Think o' the splendid show you 're agoin' to see. Look, here 's our Hiram goin' to give ye one o' his lozengers; spearmint, too; ye know ye love spearmint lozengers."

At this moment we were borne away from the Butterfield family by the swaying crowd, and we saw them no more.

After we were safely seated, Mr. Jack Hamlin suddenly became silent. He made no more jests, and if I turned to speak to him, I found him regarding me with a curious glance that I could not understand.

"What is it?" I asked, involuntarily putting up my hands to straighten my hat. "Am I very untidy? You know I was not dressed at all to go anywhere."

"It is not that," he said, still looking at me; "it is only that I am a selfish brute. I had no business to persuade you to come to the circus. They'll all be down on you when we get back."

"Oh, I shall not mind," I said cheerfully; "I don't care a bit for Lucretia's scoldings."

"It is not only Lucretia who will disapprove," he returned. "They will all be down on you, and it is entirely my fault."

"I'll go home now if you wish," I said reluctantly.

"We may as well stay, now we are here," he replied; then he laughed suddenly.

"I believe you actually care about this beggarly circus!" he exclaimed.

I did care, though Mr. Jack Hamlin despised it. I liked it all. Everything was new to me, and I laughed at even the clown's stale jests, and was completely deceived by the time-worn trick of the unbroken donkey. I was really sorry when the "show" was over, and we were once more on the dusty road which led toward home. Before we started on our long walk, Mr. Hamlin insisted on getting me some refreshment. He left me in the cool beech wood while he crossed the bridge to the "village store." He had been gone some time when a crashing of the bushes on the bank startled me. I was afraid some rough fellow from the circus grounds had seen me, and my breath came easier when I saw the dark young man who rode the bicycle.

"I beg your pardon," he said, raising his hat, "but you see I remembered that we were companions in misfortune the day of the thunder-storm. I wonder if I dare ask a great favor of you."

He had taken off his hat; and as he stood leaning against a beech-tree and looking down upon me, I thought I had never imagined so handsome a man.

"You do not look very stony-hearted," he said.

"I would do it," I said, blushing stupidly, "if I were sure — "

"There is no harm in it," he said quickly; "see, it is only to give this note, quite privately, to Miss Alexander, at the camp."

"To Miss Alexander!" I exclaimed in sur-prise by no means well-bred.

"If you will be so very kind," he said, hand-ing me the letter, which was written on a sheet torn from a note-book.

"May I also ask you to add to my obligation by letting this be a secret, a *secret à trois?*"

"I will not tell," I said stupidly.

I could not think of anything graceful to say. I was surprised and startled, and felt more than ever before like an awkward, clumsy country girl. Suddenly, before I knew it, the young man bent and kissed my hand.

"You are so good," he said devoutly. "Keep the faith," and crashed away through the bushes. Mr. Hamlin appeared at the same moment with his hands full of packages.

"All the luxuries of the season," he began gayly.

Then he stopped abruptly, looking from me to the disappearing figure of the stranger.

"What did he want? Did he speak to you?" he demanded.

"Yes, he spoke," I said, blushing under my questioner's uncomfortably keen eyes. "He — did not say much."

"I wish to know what he said to you," said Mr. Jack Hamlin, imperiously.

"I shall not tell," I said sternly. "I — I promised not."

"You promised that fellow," said Mr. Hamlin, incredulously.

"Yes," I said; "it was no harm, and it concerns — I will not tell you anything about it," I broke off angrily. "You stand there as if you were my judge. I shall not say another word about it."

"Very well, do exactly as you please," said Mr. Hamlin, coldly.

He sat down, but he was quite white and grim, and his eyebrows were drawn together in an ugly frown. He opened his various parcels, but there was no longer any fun about the little picnic. I was too disturbed to eat, and we soon gave it up and started silently for home. I was unhappy enough, but I could not break my promise; and after all, Mr. Jack Hamlin had no right to question me as if he were my father. We plodded along the sunny, warm high-road

for about a mile in most uncomfortable com-
panionship ; then a wagon overtook us. It
contained only a farmer and his sallow, tired
wife.

" Won't you have a lift ? " asked the woman.
" We 're goin' along quite a piece, — way past
the Farrar deestrick."

" Thank you," said Mr. Hamlin; " I think
this young lady will be very glad to ride. I
am sure you must be tired of walking," he
added with a peculiar emphasis, turning to me.

" I should be very glad to ride," I said
viciously.

If Mr. Jack Hamlin wished to be rid of me,
at least he should not find it a difficult task.
In a moment I was in the wagon, and Mr.
Hamlin, lifting his hat rather too deferentially,
had started off at a pace which promised to
bring him into camp long before me.

XIX.

WHAT BETTY SAYS.

"WHERE do they keep the sun when it rains?" asked Bevis Sparhawk, plaintively; and some older persons than Bevis wondered how Nature could get up so complete a transformation in so short a time. The hapless day of the circus was clear and warm and gracious; the next day dawned gray and cold, with a lowering sky, and a raw wind that chilled one to the marrow. The camp-fire was the only cheerful feature of the landscape, and around this we all huddled, pretending to be neither cold nor hungry. Mrs. Sparhawk wrote a letter upon thin foreign paper. Mrs. Winthrop tried to mend her husband's stockings, her fingers stiff with cold. Some read, and some played whist. Miss Alexander played chess with Mr. Hamlin.

She did not look blue and pinched like the rest
of us. She looked unusually fascinating. She
wore a warm gown of dark blue and red in wide
stripes, and had a boyish jacket and a little fez
of knitted silk. Mr. Hamlin was almost hidden
in his ulster, and looked cross and dismal.

As for me, I not only was frowned upon by
the weather, but by everybody in the camp.
Everybody disapproved of me, and I felt that I
had done a deed only once removed from mur-
der, in going to the circus. Lucretia had been
" shocked," and Mrs. Winthrop " surprised,"
and Mrs. Dudley knew I would be ill. Mrs.
Sparhawk majestically disapproved of me, and
Josephine was spiteful. Miss Alexander told
me I was a " darling love," when I delivered my
private despatch; and Mr. Hamlin, after freeing
me from the responsibility of our escapade, had
entirely ignored me, as if by speaking to the
bicycle man I had forever lowered myself in
his royal favor. The children only remained

my friends, and I was reduced to the not very lively amusement of tracing pictures on Rodney's transparent slate for his edification.

"A salad," said Colonel Sparhawk, from the other side of the fire, "should never be cut. Upon my soul, sir, when I see a vandal touch a knife to a plate of lettuce or cress, I — I want to annihilate him, sir; I do, upon my word."

"I wonder," said mild Mrs. Winthrop, from her mending, "why it is that we all have such a tendency to talk about food. It seems to be almost the only subject that really interests us."

"It is because we are starving," said Emily Dudley, boldly but hoarsely. "We have n't had anything *real* to eat for three weeks. We all of us loathe eggs and abhor fish, only we don't dare to say so; and we are starving for a bit of meat, only we 'd die before we owned it."

She sneezed violently several times, and was pounced upon by her mother and borne away to be dosed.

"She has told the truth," said Mr. Winthrop, with tragic solemnity; "we are starving."

"Is that true?" asked Mr. Hamlin; "are we starving? Are you starving, Miss Betty?"

He had not spoken to me before that day, and he turned to me so suddenly that he took away my breath.

"Yes," I admitted coldly, "I am like the rest."

He turned back to his chess looking as cross as ever. Rodney Sparhawk, having been sent to his mother's desk for a postage-stamp, now appeared gracefully bearing one upon the tip of his outstretched tongue.

"All licked, Mamma!" he announced with cheerful vulgarity.

"I say, Betty," called Bob, "how much did our turkey weigh last Thanksgiving? He was a buster, I tell you. Don't I just wish we had him now, though!"

The day grew every minute more chill and

dismal. Mr. Hamlin, having finished his game, disappeared. Lucretia and Josephine sought for comfort in the tent. Bobby and Fred replenished the fire, and then challenged me to a game of " stick knife." It was after quite half an hour's silence that Mrs. Sparhawk looked up abstractedly.

" Does anybody smell smoke? " she asked, — " not the fire, but as if cloth of some sort were burning? Colonel, go and see if either of your children is afire. Pray do not sit there in that unconcerned manner, as if you did not care."

The Colonel looked up and dropped his cards.

" Why, my dear life ! " he exclaimed, " you are burning yourself. I assure you the tail of your gown is all afire."

A thin blue line of smoke was indeed rising over Mrs. Sparhawk's left shoulder, and her gown was really smouldering. It was extinguished in a moment, and Mrs. Sparhawk's face was as completely unruffled as if the occurrence were too commonplace to rouse even surprise.

"Wodney did it! Wodney did it!" shouted Bevis, with all the holy joy of bringing a criminal to justice. "Wodney had a catty-nintle, and he sticked it in the fire and so he blazed your dress, he did."

The Colonel, more angry than he was often seen, bore Rodney away to meet some unknown awful fate, while Bevis looked on with placid approval.

"I wouldn't burn you, would I, Mamma?" he asked, with the conscious virtue of one child who beholds another in disgrace.

"Yes, I dare say you would," answered his mother; "in fact, I dare say you did do it, just now, and not Rodney at all. Where is Rodney?"

"In the dining tent," replied Bevis, with unmistakable relish. "I guess Papa'll give him a norful wippin'."

" You nasty little vindictive thing! " Mrs. Sparhawk exclaimed. " Go at once and tell Papa that I will not have Rodney punished. It will ruin his disposition. Hurry, or I will tell him to give you a good beating."

Thus spurred on, Bevis flew away, losing off his little red fez and dropping a cherished lapful of stones. His place was taken at once by Mr. Jack Hamlin.

" To Starvation Camp — with the compliments of the archer," he said, and tossed down upon the wet grass half a dozen well-grown fowls.

They were plainly domestic, were still in their feathers, and each one was pierced through the neck with mathematical precision by a Highfield arrow of the very best sort.

" Where did they come from? " cried a chorus of voices.

" They came from the farm," replied Mr. Hamlin, boldly. " There is no game anywhere else. It is all right. I did n't steal them."

"Oh, of course not," said Mr. Winthrop; "but," he added feebly, "the rule of our camp, you know, did — you shoot them?"

"Of course he did," Mr. Dudley put in sharply; "can't you see the arrows?"

Involuntarily every person about the fire exchanged sneaking glances with every other. Guilt was written plainly upon every countenance. A painful silence fell upon us. It was broken by Rodney Sparhawk, who appeared cheerful and unharmed from his encounter with his father.

"I would like *all* the drumsticks, if you please; and Bevis can have the necks," he remarked generously.

"Is he not a nasty little pig?" cried Mrs. Sparhawk; "but do we not all feel exactly like him?"

"I would propose," said Mrs. Winthrop, "a luncheon of coffee and bread and cheese, and then a nice hot dinner at four or five o'clock."

This being unanimously agreed upon, some plates of wilted hardbread and a box of mouldy cheese were produced. These Mr. Winthrop persisted in calling " the relics," and indeed the sight of them has become tolerably familiar. However, by the aid of hot coffee, we did our duty, and declared that we had enjoyed our luncheon. Who would not be amiable with those blissful chickens in view?

" I would n't be ungallant for the world," remarked Theodore, mildly; " but perhaps you may have heard what class of people don't know enough to go in when it rains."

" Why, so it is raining, really ! " cried everybody.

The mist had thickened to a steady drizzle.

" Let us go to the dining tent and play games," proposed Arthur Winthrop. " I know a very amusing thing, very laughable. We used to do it at church sociables."

" It must be highly amusing, then," grumbled

Ted; but we all rose and bore wraps and books into the tent.

"Now," began Arthur, cheerfully beaming upon us through his blinking glasses, "this is a game of sneezing, you know. We will begin at the end of the row. You, Fred, must say 'hish,' Lucretia must say 'hash,' and Betty must say 'hosh.' Miss Alexander must say 'hish,' and so on all around. I'll drop my handkerchief, and then you must all speak together."

"Hosh!" said Mr. Dudley, loudly and prematurely.

"I had not dropped the handkerchief," said Arthur, looking mildly reproachful. "Now, be ready, everybody."

The handkerchief dropped, and a chorus of hishes and hoshes filled the air. Silence followed, during which we all gazed vaguely at each other.

"What do we do next?" asked Mr. Hamlin, briskly.

"You don't do anything next," replied Arthur,
"that's it; that's the game."

"Oh," said Mr. Hamlin, blandly.

"Don't you see?" poor Arthur urged, becoming rather pink in the face; "it represents a
gigantic sneeze."

"Very amusing, I'm sure," ventured Miss
Alexander, smiling.

"I think I'll go and take a siesta," said Mrs.
Sparhawk, cruelly. "Rodney, you and Bevis
may come, too."

Mrs. Sparhawk's example was followed by
the older ladies and Emily Dudley. The rest
of us remained to play a stupid game called
"Doctrines," which was also under the leader-
ship of Arthur Winthrop; indeed, Arthur chiefly
excelled in games. Finally even our patience
was exhausted. We withdrew, leaving the gentlemen to their own devices. It was now raining
steadily, and in our big tent we found Mrs. Sparhawk reading a German novel. Pretty Bevis

was asleep in a hammock, while Rodney on the floor was peacefully cutting dogs and horses out of his mother's prayer-book. Emily Dudley sat huddled up on her little bed with her waterproof about her. She was trying to read, but looked out of temper and thoroughly disgusted with life. As we came in she shut her book with a clap.

"I am tired of it," she said vehemently. "I am tired of sleeping on damp straw, with a grasshopper down my neck and a spider in my ear. I'm tired of pretending that my feet are not wet and my face is not burnt to a blister. I am sick of eating bugs and drinking caterpillars. I hate the very sight of fish, and I never want to see another egg as long as I live. I won't pretend any longer. I want to go home, and I want to go now. There!"

We could not have been more taken off our feet if old Sippican had spoken. It was so unexpected an outburst to come from sensible, matter-of-fact Emily Dudley, that we simply stood in a group and stared at her.

" Where is your mother? " weakly asked Josephine at length.

" Gone to help Mrs. Winthrop with the chickens," replied Emily, stonily; " but you need not call her. I am not sick. I am only tired of starving in this nasty camp."

" Your sentiments do you credit," laughed Mrs. Sparhawk. " You feel exactly as we all do, only nobody else has the courage to speak. I admire you."

" Cheer up, Emmy," said Lucretia, " I have just had a piece of news. We are all invited to a dance in a new barn, at the Bascoms', beyond the mountain. Won't that be fine for Thursday night? "

" I thought it was Wednesday," said Miss Alexander.

" Why, how could you know anything about it? " asked Lucretia, with astonished blue eyes.

"Bobby this minute brought down the invitation from the farm-house."

"I meant that I *wished* it were Wednesday night," corrected Miss Alexander, flushing oddly.

XX.

WHAT BOB SAYS.

BETTY need n't brag so. She puts on great airs that she has written more than I have, and all that; but she did n't have to spend all her time fishing and getting berries, as Fred and I have. Beside, Betty need n't feel so everlasting big for her writing, for she has n't told everything just as it happened. Hamlin gave me a first-class jointed fishing-rod, and Fred said he only did it because he was spooney about Betty. I never thought anybody could get spooney over her, and I don't more than half believe it now; but, all the same, she is n't honest Injun when she writes, for she leaves out about Mr. Hamlin, — the lilies he brought her, and the rows in the punt, and candy from New York her birthday. She does n't tell everything.

We've had one square meal; brown fricassee of chicken, and baked potatoes, green corn, shelled beans and hot biscuit, apple-pie and cheese and coffee, — the first meat we've seen for weeks, and perhaps we were n't hungry, though! Betty says not to tell what we have to eat; says it's vulgar; but I took notice she was glad enough to eat her share of the chicken.

I took a note round the mountain to the bicycle fellow from Miss Alexander. She cried and said I was her only friend. It was out behind the dining tent. I felt like a fool, but I took the note. Something is queer about it all. We are going to a barn dance. She makes a fellow do just as she wants him to.

XXI.

WHAT BETTY SAYS.

"I NEVER can get in," sighed Josephine; "never in the world."

"Oh," encouraged Lucretia, "yes, you can. It is not high at all, and the straw is lovely."

We were all piling, with much fun and laughter, into the Farrars' big hay-rack. Mrs. Farrar, a meek and depressed-looking woman, was already seated, while her husband stood ready to drive the stout, bony gray horses.

"Come," urged Fred, bluntly, "hurry up, Jo. We have n't too much time, and barn dances don't wait for anybody. Here, I 'll boost you."

"Go away, Fred," said Josephine, sharply; but she took Arthur Winthrop's hand, and, with some lady-like small shrieks, at length was in and seated.

Rodney and Bevis sat on either side of me.

"Don't you think I 'm very still?" the former asked, before we were fairly started.

"Why, yes, Rodney," I assented.

"I 've got to be still for a whole hour," he answered sadly. "Then Mr. Hamlin will give me a silver dollar. He said he would."

"I 'll be still for five hundred dollars," put in Bevis, promptly, rising heavily over Rodney's price.

"Annie Alexander," exclaimed Mrs. Sparhawk, "I asked you to wear your white wool gown, and there you are, as prim as a nun, in that dark-gray."

"I thought this was more suitable," answered Miss Alexander, pleasantly, as she drew on her long, gray Swedish gloves.

She rose presently and came over to me, displacing Bevis, who openly objected. It was already quite dusky, so that we could scarcely see from end to end of the cart.

"Miss Betty," said Miss Alexander, softly, "we are going to break camp to-morrow, you know, and I shall be going away. You have n't liked me very well, but I took a fancy to you the first time I ever saw you. I have few friends, and my life is not very happy. You have been kind to me, and I think you did not like the secrecy of that note; but, indeed, it was necessary. I am so persecuted and so un-happy. I do not want you to quite forget me, child. You must wear this. I brought it home from Rome. Please do not say no; I am so miserable, so frightened."

She rose, and hastily returned to her seat by the side of Mr. Hamlin. A moment later I heard her teaching him a Spanish song, and laughing quite merrily over his bad pronuncia-tion. She had put a ring on the third finger of my hand. I could just see it in the dusk, and it felt rough with engraving. I did not wish to make a scene in the hay-cart, but I promised myself that I would give it back as soon as we reached the barn. I did not want any of her rings or her mysteries.

It was a delicious evening, dry and warm. The air was full of wild scents of elder and rank brakes and sweet-fern. Later the moon would come, but then it was dusk, which deepened to midnight whenever we passed through a wood. Along the sides of the road the fireflies were holding a glittering dance on their own account.

" Cuddle me up," said Bevis, tumbling suddenly into my lap; " I 'm 'fraid o' the bears."

" I 'm goin' to holler awful loud when I get me silver dollar," presently confided Rodney, who really had been surprisingly well-behaved for him.

" Oh, Rodney," I said entreatingly.

" And squeal," said Rodney, with the joy of coming triumph in his voice, " and stamp and run all wound and wound, and do a norful lot of kinds of things; you wait and see."

" Me, too," said Bevis; " I 'll do some norful things, too."

I did not doubt the children's ability, but I was prevented from delivering them a lecture by our arrival at the farm. The great new barn towered white in the dusk, and the farmer came out to meet us.

" How de do? How de do? " he said cordially. " Glad to see yer. We haint goin' to make no strangers of ye. Come right in, all on ye, and make yourselves to home."

Within the barn a fiddle was twanging, played by a weazened old man sitting on a barrel. There were neither cattle nor hay. The barn was quite new, and smelled of sweet pine-wood. There were candles everywhere in bottles, and upon boards pierced with rows of holes. The two great doors stood open to the wide, cool night. From the back door we saw the orchard, and behind the dark, rustling trees we saw the great red moon just rising.

As we went in, a dozen pairs of young people were dancing a " French Four." Some farmers' wives sat on rude benches against the wall, and a group of men stood talking by the door. Fred came at once to ask me to dance, and we were soon merrily flying "down the centre."

Adaline Butterfield, smiling and awkward, was next me in the long line. She told me regretfully that " the boarder " had gone back to the Gorge, but had " given mother an elegant shawl," and herself " a pair of earrings."

The " French Four " was followed by a " Boston Fancy," and that by a " Virginia Reel." We became hilarious, and sometimes went not only " down the centre " of the barn, but rushed pell-mell into the dewy field outside.

Lucretia and Josephine considered such dancing rude, but I am hoyden enough to enjoy a dance that has some life in it. I danced chiefly with Bobby and Fred. Mr. Jack Hamlin stood leaning against the wall looking cross. Miss Alexander danced, and in spite of her dull gray gown was the most brilliant woman in the room. Her cheeks were as pink as a sea-shell, and her eyes had a lovely starry look.

Presently I found myself standing by the door, after a wild polka with Bob. Mr. Hamlin came across and joined me.

" What are you thinking? " I asked.

" Of what happens to the best-laid plans," he answered.

" Have your plans gone agley? "

" Did n't you know they had? "

"Why, no," I said stupidly; " how did they?"

" I will tell you going home," he said, " if you do not have the entire Sparhawk family in your lap. I may be able to sit next you."

" You can talk if you do not sit next me," I said cheerfully. " I 'm sure I talked to Bobby all the way over, and he sat quite at the other end of the cart."

"I heard you," he said dryly. "I don't care to shout."

Just at this moment up came Rodney Sparhawk begging me to dance with him.

"Why, Rodney," said his mother, "you do not know how to dance. What are you thinking of?"

"Yes, I do know how," insisted Rodney, stoutly. "I know 'swing pardners' and 'down the centre.'"

"Rodney, this is all nonsense," declared Mrs. Sparhawk, decidedly. "Once for all, I forbid your trying to dance. Do you understand?"

"If you don't let me," said Rodney, calmly, "I'm afraid I shall holler and roar and run between the dancing people, and knock 'em all down."

Mrs. Sparhawk adjusted her eyeglasses and gazed a moment at her son.

"Very well, you disagreeable child," she said, "go along then and make a nasty little guy of yourself, and set everybody laughing at you, if you want to. I only hope you may not kill Miss Betty."

Indeed, Rodney did make a guy, not only of himself but of me; for he knew none of the changes, and had to be pushed and pulled about in a shameful manner. He enjoyed himself immensely, however, and went down the centre riotously, usually tumbling down at the end and being ignominiously picked up and set on end again by the nearest person. I was still alive when the dance ended, but not much more.

"I have been observing the various elegant ways of inviting a lady to dance," said Mr. Hamlin, strolling up to me as I sat quite exhausted on the bench by the door.

"And how do they do it?" inquired Mrs. Sparhawk, joining us. "Miss Betty, please have my fan. I am sure you are in a fainting condition."

"One gentleman," said Mr. Hamlin, "crooks

his elbow and offers his arm without a word; another — that white-haired one with the green cravat — says, 'Dance longer me?' and a third says, 'Darse to dance this dance with me?' I have watched the last gentleman through a Virginia reel, and I admit that it does require a certain amount of courage to be his partner."

"How unique!" said Mrs. Sparhawk, only faintly amused. "Have you seen Miss Alexander lately? I am forgetting that I am her chaperone."

"She is by the other door with Ted," he replied indifferently.

"What is the matter with my crimps, Betty, can you see?" asked Josephine, who had been trying to polka with Arthur Winthrop.

"You seem to have a pair of eyeglasses tangled in your hair," said Mrs. Sparhawk, nonchalantly, as if the thing were of common occurrence.

"How detestable!" said Josephine, without

smiling. "They are Arthur Winthrop's. He is blind as a bat without them, and he is too absurdly polite to ask me for them. How silly he is!"

After much dancing there was a supper in the big farm kitchen, and not long after, our hay-rack was announced as ready for the homeward trip.

"Pile in," shouted Bobby, jovially; "I've shaken up the cushions, and the chariot is ready. They've given us heaps of apples."

"Look out for worms, though," suggested Fred, unpleasantly; "eating early apples in the dark is n't what it's cracked up to be."

There was some attempt at singing as we started away, but presently we grew sleepy and silent. Bevis came to me and went to sleep in my arms. Rodney insisted on driving.

"Rodney Sparhawk," cried his mother, "if you run over my feet once more I'll assassinate you. Come away from the reins at once, and stop troubling Mr. Farrar. Do you hear me? Rodney Sparhawk, why don't you answer me?"

" I 'm not listening to you at all, Mamma," replied Rodney, serenely; " I am looking at the moon."

Mrs. Sparhawk sighed and composed herself for a nap.

We came after a time to the Butterfield farm, where we had taken refuge from the storm. Late as it was, the house door stood open, and the light from within streaming out into the yard showed a group standing about a chaise, from which the horse had been taken.

" Somebody must be sick," said Mrs. Dudley. " Let us stop."

" They must be in some trouble," Mrs. Winthrop agreed. " Some of you young and active ones had better see if we can be of any help."

We found the entire Butterfield family in the yard, except Adaline, who was to pass the night at the farm where the dance was given. Even the shy Elnathan had come forth, owl-like, under cover of the night.   In the shadow of the chaise-top we could see by the moonlight a small old woman in a decent black bonnet and shawl. She was sitting stiffly upright, with folded hands and a forbidding expression of countenance.

" It is his mother," explained Mrs. Butterfield, in a low tone.   " She stops about to her differ-ent children's, a spell here an' a spell there. She haint raly well-witted by times; not that she 's crazy, but she 's notionate, an', — wal, she 's sort o' cur'us, mother is.   She gits an idea in her head, an' then she sorter can't seem to git red of it."

" What is the matter with her now? " inquired Bobby.

" Wal, ye see she 's come over to stop a spell along of us.   Elnathan went over to his Aunt Emma Jane's ternoon to fetch her.   They got here jest at tea-time, an' Mother, she 's took a notion not to stir from that shay.   Elnathan,

he's ontackled, an' we've all ben a coaxin' of
her in ever sence six o'clock, an' there that
contr'y old lady has sot an' sot, as ef she'd
took root."

"Maria," said the old woman, suddenly interrupting, "go into the house. You make me
fidgety."

"But, Mother," urged Mrs. Butterfield, "the
dew is rale heavy, an' it's a cool night. You'll
have rheumatics to-morrow, sure as preachin'."

"If I do, Maria," returned the old woman,
with dignity, "it will be my own lookout,
Maria."

"But, Granny, you are keepin' us out-doors
all night," urged Elnathan.

"I am not aweer," said the grandmother, with
rigid politeness, "that I have asked any of you
to stop out o' door. If I hev, will somebody
please to tell me?"

"Come, Mother, come," said poor Mrs. Butterfield, "it's nigh onto midnight, an' a nice

bed all made an' waitin' for ye in the parlor bedroom."

" I 'm puffeckly comfortable where I be, Maria, an' I don't know why I should n't stay here."

" Mother made sweet cake an' blueberry pie a purpose for ye," put in one of the children, " an' she 's cut into a new sage-cheese, an' kep' the tea on all this time."

" If I have lived," said the old lady, frigidly, " to have the few things that my own folks do for me throwed up in my face, I may ez wal go to the Poor Farm an' done with it. I never thought to see myself looked on as a burden to my own son's house; that I will raise my Ebenezer to say."

"Nobuddy ever thought of castin' things up at you. Now, Mother, you know better than that," said her daughter-in-law. " Dear sakes, if *he* had only got home, he could manage her; but he won't come till to-morrow. I declare, I don't know which way to turn."

"You never did, Maria," the old lady commented from her chaise. "You was always unfaculized and hen-headed, an' so I told Simeon when he first began to keep company with ye. He was headstrong, an' hev his own way he would, but he'll come to repent on it, ef he has n't already."

"Oh, Granny," cried one of the children, running from the house, "there's our Mirandy, she's gone and opened your band-box, and she's tried on your best cap, and is pulling out all your things, and I can't make her stop nohow."

"Land sakes," said the old lady, excitedly, "ef that child aint exactly like you, Maria, always interferin' an' meddlin'. My best cap! All that purple taste! Elnathan, help me outen this shay, an' I'll soon put a bee in her bunnit."

With this the grandmother actually descended, and hurried into the house with her grandson.

"Good-night," said Mrs. Butterfield, hurriedly;

"you 'll excuse me goin' right in, but she 's so pudgicky there 's no tellin' what new notion she may take. If I can only get the door locked, we may coax her to bed. I 'm 'bleeged to ye for stoppin', I 'm sure. Good-night."

"When a woman will," laughed Colonel Sparhawk as we once more jolted along.

"*Femina semper mutabile*," added Arthur Winthrop.

"Don't be so superior," begged Mrs. Sparhawk. "Woman's power to change her mind is one of her most charming qualities. I suppose if a man had announced his intention of spending the night in a cart, he 'd have done it, if he 'd been the death of his entire family."

We reached the camp just after midnight, a sleepy and demoralized crew. After we reached our tent somebody asked for Miss Alexander.

"She was not in the cart," said Lucretia, with awful calmness; "we have gone and left her behind."

Mrs. Sparhawk, who was tucking Bevis into bed, made a sudden snatch at something on her pillow.

It was a letter.

"She has gone!" she cried wildly, "gone! Where is the Colonel? That nasty, ungrateful, theatrical little cat has eloped!"

18

XXII.

WHAT BETTY SAYS.

"SHE is a nasty, ungrateful, romantic little idiot!" declared Mrs. Sparhawk for the fortieth time since Miss Alexander's surprising escapade had been discovered the night before. "I thought she acted odd and dumpy and unlike herself, and all the time it seems that she was mooning over that lackadaisical loon of a George Dexter. Well, I wash my hands of her."

"My dearest," said the Colonel, who made one of the small group by the camp-fire who listened to this tirade, — "my dearest, pardon me; but, having taken a young lady from her parents' protection and assumed the care of her ourselves, we cannot, I think, throw off the responsibility so lightly. I feel it my duty to get a horse and go to the Gorge at once, and I think, love, that you ought to accompany me."

"Indeed, limkin, I shall do no such thing. I never want to set eyes upon her deceitful face again. To think how she apparently fell in with all my plans, and all the time she was meeting this idiot on his eternal bicycle. I wonder if they eloped on the bicycle, by the bye?"

"What does her letter say?" asked the Colonel. "Just read it to me once more, my own."

"Oh," returned Mrs. Sparhawk, airily, "I don't know where her nasty letter is, I'm sure. I dare say the children have it. She 'hoped I would try to forgive her,' and 'indeed she was very unhappy,' and she 'could not bear to deceive me and the dear Colonel, but there was no other way;' and she and Mr. Dexter had met and arranged everything, and were to be married at the house of the minister last evening. Oh, I have no patience with the little hussy; married at a country parson's house, when she might have had the loveliest wedding ever seen in Baltimore!"

"But if her parents disapproved?" began Lucretia, mildly.

"Disapproved!" cried Mrs. Sparhawk; "why, child, they've been angling for George Dexter ever since Annie was in pinafores."

"But I think she was very unhappy at home," ventured Lucretia.

"Bosh!" exclaimed Mrs. Sparhawk; "how that girl has imposed on you! Her parents idolize her. She has n't had a wish ungratified since she was born."

"The long and short of the matter," said the Colonel, "is that she is a weak, sentimental, sensational young woman, who longs to emulate the heroines of her favorite romances; so she posed for a persecuted and unhappy maiden, and really almost cheated herself into the belief that she was one. Now, my dear, I 'm off to the Gorge to see her if I can."

"Don't bring her back," cried his wife; "I will positively not see her. Think," she added, with an air of severe virtue, "of what an example to set the children!"

"Lucretia," I asked, "did she confide in you, and tell you that she was very miserable, and that her heart would break if she did not speak to somebody?"

"Why, yes," admitted Lucretia, with a somewhat injured air; "how did you know, Betty?"

"Because she said the same to me, and I carried a note from him, the circus day."

"She confided in me, too," said Emily Dudley, grimly.

"That is why she persisted in wearing a travelling dress last night," broke forth Mrs. Sparhawk, once more; "and to think of the way I put myself out for the girl. I'm sure that I wrote and invited her here the very day that I found out that Mr. Hamlin was old Judge Hamlin's nephew. I've been positively indecent in the bold-faced way I 've made opportunities for her. The Colonel has scolded me for it unmercifully. Oh, you need not open your lovely gray eyes so wide, Miss Betty; I can see through a millstone; I know where he has always been, when I did n't positively send him to Annie. Well, you may have him now, child. I shall not play the part of meddlesome Matty any longer."

As she spoke she tossed aside some bits of an envelope she had been destroying, and rising, moved slowly away, sweeping off with her long gown Emily's embroidered crewels which lay in a tiny basket on the grass. For a moment nobody spoke, but I felt all eyes upon my face. My cheeks glowed like hot coals, and my heart seemed to stop beating.

"Meddlesome Matty, I should say!" spoke out Josephine, spitefully; "what on earth does the woman mean? Her glasses must have magic in them, for she certainly sees more than the rest of us."

" I don't know that she does," said Emmy Dudley, coolly; " there are none so blind as those — You know the rest."

" You need n't trouble to explain," said Josephine, frigidly, rising and stalking off with her head in the air.

" I don't see what 's the trouble with Josephine," said Emmy, threading her needle; " I 'm sure it is none of her funeral."

Mrs. Winthrop kindly reached over and gave my hand a squeeze under her shawl, but I could not thank her. I could not speak at all. My only desire was to get away from them all; to be by myself. I could only bless the fate which had ordained that only that little circle of women had been about the fire when Mrs. Sparhawk dropped her bomb-shell.

I rose and fled — anywhere to be away from them all. I could not go to the tent, for Mrs. Sparhawk was there. I crossed the road to the meadow. I would have liked to climb the mountain and keep on and on, and never come back any more. I kept saying over and over to myself: " They thought I liked him. They all thought I liked him."

It actually seemed to me as if I should die of the horrible shame of it all. Suddenly I heard a puffing and panting close behind me.

" Oh," said Rodney's voice, " I saw you agoing to walk, so I knew you 'd want me to come too."

" No, Rodney," I said, " I am going too far. You must not come. You 'll be too tired."

" Then you can carry me a pick-a-back," persisted Rodney, cheerfully. " Besides, I 'd rather go, and I just as lief as not."

I gave the child my hand, not very pleasantly, and made my hasty steps agree better with his. After all, there was no harm in Rodney. His eyes did not pry.

" I 'll tell you sumpin'," he casually confided ; " Mr. Hamlin is up here somewhere, he and Bob."

"What do you mean?" I demanded fiercely, my cheeks flushing more hotly than ever.

He would think, they would think, I had followed him.

"Come back at once, Rodney," I said. "We will not go a step farther."

I turned and was hastening back, dragging the reluctant Rodney after me, when suddenly I saw Mr. Hamlin, with his fishing-rod, breaking his way out of the alder bushes by the brook. I drew the child down behind a friendly bowlder, and hid myself.

"Don't you speak or move, Rodney Sparhawk, till he has gone by," I whispered.

"Why not?" asked Rodney, hoarsely; "I want to see his fishes. Mamma told Papa he was a catch. What is a catch?"

"She could not have said that, Rodney."

"She did," persisted the child; "she said, 'When his uncle dies he will be a great catch.' What did she mean?"

A sudden light broke over me. How stupid I had been! Mrs. Sparhawk's graciousness to Mr. Hamlin had all been after she had learned his relationship to the rich uncle in Baltimore. If she had only heard that story that I heard in the old graveyard, she would not have wanted Miss Alexander to marry him. She would have let him alone, and not said horrible things to me, and perhaps —

"Ow!" said Rodney; "I'm a-goin' to sneeze."

"Rodney Sparhawk," I whispered fiercely, "don't you *dare* to sneeze. If you do I'll never play with you again, nor tell you another story in all my life."

Mr. Hamlin came nearer, whistling "How Can I Leave Thee," very much off key. He was just opposite our bowlder now, and, as bad luck would have it, he stopped whistling. Rodney's small face was a tangle of twists and wrinkles, as he vainly tried to overcome his desire to sneeze.

"A choo!" said Rodney, loudly. "There, Miss Betty, I couldn't help it. I couldn't, truly now."

Mr. Hamlin stepped around the corner of the rock.

"I'm sorry you've taken cold, Miss Betty," he said, "but very glad to see you. I wanted to speak to you away from the camp."

"It was Rodney who sneezed," I said stiffly; "nobody but Rodney sneezes so loudly as that. Come, Rodney, your mother will want you."

"Oh, no, she won't," replied Rodney. "She told me to stay ever so far off while she was packing."

"You may take my fishing-rod and catch a little trout. Miss Betty and I will wait for you here," said Mr. Hamlin, generously.

"Indeed he cannot, Mr. Hamlin," I cried. "Rodney is too little to go to the brook alone. Are you crazy?"

"Not now, but I may be if you won't listen

to me.   See here, Rodney, I have a secret to
tell Miss Betty, and — "

" I do not want to hear it," I cried, rising.
" I detest secrets."

" But you must hear it," he said suddenly,
very white in the face.   " Rodney, wait for us
over by that tree."

" I 'd just as lief stay," said Rodney, obligingly.
" I like to hear secrets, too."

" Rodney," exclaimed Mr. Hamlin, desperately, " if you 'll go and sit under the apple-tree
five minutes, I 'll give you a dollar."

" Honest? " asked the child.

" Of course.   I give you my word."

" All right," said Rodney, and reluctantly
departed.

I felt as if my last support had left me as he
stumbled away through the sweet fern.

" I must go," I protested ; " some other time
will do — "

" No other time will do," he said.   " I am

going home to-morrow. Betty, Mrs. Sparhawk
said that you were going to marry Arthur Winthrop. Is it true?"

"I am not going to marry anybody," I returned hotly. "I hate all this talk about marrying, as if everybody were crazy, and there were
nothing else worth thinking of."

"Oh, Betty," he said eagerly, — "oh, Betty,
Betty, don't you know how I love you? Don't
you know how I've loved you all summer,
always, ever since I was born? Betty, it cannot
be that you won't come to love me a little — "

"I came back," broke in the cheerful voice of
Rodney, "because there's a toad down there,
and I want something to poke him with. Any
picked stick would do, or your fish-pole, Mr.
Hamlin."

"Betty," said Mr. Hamlin, desperately, "I
love you utterly, but I hereby resign all hope
of telling you so out of hearing of the Sparhawk
children. It is fate. Plainly, and before this
witness, will you marry me, Betty?"

He had quite stopped smiling, and he held
both my hands in spite of Rodney. Under his
breath he said, —

"For Heaven's sake, Betty, give me an answer
before we go back to that staring camp."

"If you marry him," piped the ever-ready
Rodney, "then I s'pose he'll marry you, and
you'll have rice thrown into your ears and
down your neck, as my Aunt Helen did. Is
she goin' to marry you, Mr. Hamlin?"

"I don't know, Rodney," said Mr. Hamlin;
"ask her."

"Are you goin' to, Miss Betty?" asked the
tormenter.

"I don't know, Rodney," I began stiffly.
My lover's anxious eyes were on me, and I
weakly ended, "But I think — I am."

Then it was that Mr. Hamlin — oh, dear! I
have promised to call him Jack, and what will
Bob say; what *will* he say! — proved equal to
the emergency. I may as well tell it all, for I
never could show Bobby this chapter, anyway;

but without a word of warning he caught Rodney's Tam-o'-Shanter by the edge and pulled it completely over the poor fellow's face, and then he took me in his arms like a flash, and I could not help it if he did kiss me like a young tornado.

"Oh, stop!" gurgled Rodney, as, half crying, he extricated himself from his cap; "that is n't any fair."

"I beg your pardon, Rodney," Mr. Hamlin said with the greatest gravity, "but you see I got hold of the edge of your cap instead of my own all by mistake."

"I don't care," protested Rodney, looking abused; "I don't like mistakes."

"Nor I, Rodney," said I, with an attempt at propriety.

"Very well," rejoined my shameless lover, without looking in the least penitent; "I 'll never do it again, Betty — by mistake."

I laughed a little. It was all so wonderful,

and I was so very happy. Rodney joined boisterously in my laughter, without knowing why he laughed.

We stood there in the damp meadow among the brambles, with Rodney eager and watchful by our side. Was ever a love-making more prosaic? Had it not been for Mr. Hamlin's eyes one could not have guessed that it was a love-making at all. We stood there in the foggy morning and regarded each other half whimsically. The whole thing was so funny, so lacking in poetry and sentiment.

" I cannot think what Bob will say," I said at length. " I always loved Bob more than all the world; and you know we were to keep house in Mexico."

" You can do that still," he smiled; " only now Bob will be the boarder, and I shall be the householder."

" Come," urged Rodney, " if you 've settled your talkin', do come and let 's poke the toad."

"Our talking is only begun," replied Mr. Hamlin, swinging the child to his shoulders; "but we have our lifetime in which to finish it. I can afford to be patient for a little now; and after all, I might not have had a chance to speak to you, my Betty, if Rodney had not sneezed."

And we all went to poke the toad.

19